THE

WAKING

HOUR

Every man has a weakness... His was strength
A Screenplay by: Chad Bailey

 www.trafford.com

North America & international
toll-free: 1 888 232 4444 (USA & Canada)
phone: 250 383 6864 ♦ fax: 812 355 4082

MUTINOUS

VEXON

QUADACALYPSE

TITLE CARD:

'MUTINOUS VEXON QUADACALYPSE'

FADE IN:

EXT. CITY STREETS - DAY

'MUTINOUS VEXON QUADACALYPSE' is shot in black and white. We PAN across a gray sky and reveal an old apartment building with a cargo truck in front of it. Soldiers are departing the truck and charging fiercely into the building.

CLOSE UP: An officer stares coldly at the camera, then walks away and enters the building with other soldiers whom charge into the premises.

INT. ALURICH AND FREYA'S BEDROOM - DAY

Alurich and Freya live in this building. They are a married couple in their twenties. Their bedroom is old and plain. Alurich is standing by the window looking out at the attack taking place on their building by the soldiers dressed in black. Freya is in bed under the covers.

FREYA

What's going on?

ALURICH

They're here. Get ready

INT. APARTMENT BUILDING - DAY

The soldiers are charging through the old building violently as they break into apartments. The occupants scream in terror.

INT. ALURICH AND FREYA'S ROOM - DAY

Alurich and Freya are both fully dressed in jeans and shirts. They gather their possessions.

CLOSE UP: BLACK BOOTS RUNNING UP STAIRS

INT. ALURICH AND FREYA'S ROOM - DAY

Alurich and Freya continue to gather their possessions. Alurich grabs his welder's kit and Freya grabs her paintings.

                    FREYA

          Lock the Door

Alurich locks the door and walks back over to Freya. Five soldiers break down the door and enter the room fully armed.

                    SOLDIER

          Come on! Let's go!

The soldiers completely destroy the room and take anything valuable. Alurich and Freya are forced out of the room by the soldiers. The young couple hangs on to their belongings.

EXT. APARTMENT BUILDING - DAY

There is a crowd of captured people standing outside the apartment building. Gunshots and screams are heard coming from the apartment building. The soldiers force the people into their cargo trucks and drive away.

EXT. TRAIN - DAY

Alurich and Freya, along with several others, stand by an old wooden trailer. A soldier flings the trailer door open.

> SOLDIER
>
> Get on my train!

The soldiers force the people into the trailer.

INT. TRAILER - DAY

Alurich and Freya sit on the crammed trailer floor with other captured citizens. All of the confused people hold on to their belongings in fear.

> FREYA
>
> Do you know what's going on?

> ALURICH
>
> I don't know

A crazy wild eyed old man is sitting by Freya.

> FREYA
>
> Excuse me sir, do you have any idea where we are going?

> OLD MAN
>
> Where are we going? We are going to die!

The old man starts laughing wildly and a soldier standing by the trailer door laughs sarcastically at the comment. Freya becomes terrified and begins to whimper.

> SOLDIER
>
> You! Quiet! No crying on my train

Alurich and Freya lie against the wall and gradually fall asleep over a span of time. Suddenly, the trailer door flings open and the sunlight is revealed.

SOLDIER (CONT'D)

> Get off my train. All of you get off my train
> now!

EXT. NORDFELS CAMP - DAY

The soldiers force the people off of the train and they enter the camp. Mozart is playing through speakers connected to wooden poles above the campsite. We fade up on Colonel Hugo Snyder, a German, late thirties, lean, goatee, cold steel gray eyes and light hair wearing a black uniform dressed to perfection. He stands on deck facing everyone.

SNYDER

> Hello, welcome to Nordfels. I am the
> commandant of this camp Colonel Hugo K.
> Snyder. As you can see, there are two groups,
> one to the right consisting of females and
> another to the left consisting of males. It is
> exactly 11:13 am. We have a long day ahead of
> us. The officers will take you to your quarters
> and in no time you will feel right at home.
> Thank you for your time

The soldiers begin moving the captives through the gates. The prisoners show the soldiers their proof of eligibility. A soldier grabs Freya's paintings and slashes through them with his knife. He throws them to the ground and pushes her over to the women's side. The soldiers separate the men and the women into two groups. A soldier comes running to Snyder.

SOLDIER

Colonel Snyder sir, the left is flooded. There
isn't enough room

SNYDER

Double check the list. If there isn't enough
room move the men to section C

SOLDIER

(Shouting) May I ask that all of the men please
separate into two lines!

The men separate into two lines and are escorted through the camp
gates. Alurich and Freya stare at each other in confusion.

SOLDIER #2

Now the women

The women are escorted through the camp gates.

SOLDIER #2 (CONT'D)

Nice and steady. Very good

INT. SNYDER'S OFFICE - DAY

A soft tap hits the door lightly. A young, skinny soldier stands by the
door with a camera strapped around his neck and a piece of paper in
his hand.

JANSDALTER

Hello, I was sent here to see a Colonel Hugo
Snyder

SNYDER

Who are you sir?

JANSDALTER

I am Corporal Cedric Jansdalter. They told me
to come here to see you sir

SNYDER

Who told you?

JANSDALTER

Gen...General Haku sir

SNYDER

I'm sorry, my apologies, I am Hugo Snyder, the
commandant of this camp. You must be the
photographer I sent for, correct?

JANSDALTER

Thank you, yes sir

Snyder takes a black lacquer watch with a Tao on the face out of his
pocket and opens it. The watch plays delicate harmonic chimes.
Snyder kisses the watch and puts it back into his pocket.

SNYDER

Come with me young sir. I will show you
around camp

EXT. SECTION A - DAY

Snyder and Jansdalter walk around Section A.

SNYDER

This is Nordfels. I helped design this camp.
You will find that it is very beneficial for its

purpose. The camp is divided into three parts. The first of which is section A. This is where the male partrons stay. As you can see there are 17 barracks. Each barrack has its own specific purpose, one through four are for sleeping, five through ten are working barracks, and eleven through fifteen are for storage. Barrack sixteen is the kitchen. Barrack seventeen is for sanitation; here you find showers and toilets for our male patrons. Come, I will show you where the women stay

EXT. SECTION B - DAY

Snyder and Jansdalter walk around Section B.

> ### SNYDER
>
> This is section B, where the women stay. It is not quite the size of section A because there aren't as many women as the men. Here, we only have eight barracks. The first three are where the female patrons live and sleep. Barracks four through six are working barracks. All possessions are taken from everyone to resell. Barrack seven is for sanitation and eight is our largest storage facility. Time is running short. Quickly, let's go to section C

EXT. SECTION C - DAY

Snyder and Jansdalter enter Section C.

> ### SNYDER
>
> Section C is the death camp. We distance

section C from the others so that our patrons
will not be frightened

JANSDALTER

Death camp, what do you mean?

SNYDER

Our totalitarian government has placed us here
as a top secret organization. Our duty, to kill
the occupants of this former land

JANSDALTER

What? But...that's illegal

SNYDER

Legality is strictly superficial. Now we make the
decisions.

Snyder and Jansdalter walk over to a large building and enter.

INT. GAS CHAMBER - DAY

Jansdalter and Snyder enter the chamber. Five dead bodies lie on the
floor. An officer is standing by the door.

JANSDALTER

This is sickening

SNYDER

This chamber is used for any clients we have
no use for. As you can see it looks much like
the shower facilities. This is used much to our
advantage. Corporal Haas

HAAS

Yes sir

SNYDER

What is this mess? There are bodies lying on the
ground, the walls are covered with grime

HAAS

I'm sorry sir. We attempted to get the chamber
cleaned after the shipment this morning, but I
haven't had time sir

SNYDER

Time? I'm tired of excuses. I want results. If
this chamber isn't cleaned promptly there may
be a malfunction, you know this. Do you
understand?

HAAS

Yes sir, I will get to work on it right away sir

Haas walks away.

SNYDER

Come with me

Snyder and Jansdalter walk over to the chamber door.

SNYDER (CONT'D)

Look at this glass inside the door. It is
unbreakable and sound proof. This allows us to
watch the clients die without having to interact
with them. Go ahead, try to break it

Jansdalter lightly taps the glass with his knuckles.

SNYDER (CONT'D)

You can hit harder than that. Here, use the gun

Snyder takes the assault rifle out of Haas's grasp and hands it to

Jansdalter. He takes the gun and hits the glass, but is once again unsuccessful.

SNYDER (CONT'D)

(Tapping the glass) Unbreakable

EXT. SECTION C - DAY

SNYDER

Well Mr. Jansdalter, I have shown you everything. Your first assignment is take pictures of everything at this camp, every building, every room, every tower, trap, and fencing. You are a talented photographer, yes?

JANSDALTER

Yes, I am sir

SNYDER

Good, Officer Pendengrob will be the one whom you will be training with this week. Don't worry about finding him, he will find you. Begin your assignment. Any questions?

Jansdalter doesn't say anything.

SNYDER (CONT'D)

Good day sir

Snyder walks away.

INT. SECTION A, BARRACK ONE - NIGHT

Alurich is thrown into the barrack by two soldiers. The barrack is crammed with prisoners. A rugged looking middle-aged black man dressed in a gray striped prisoner's garb leisurely walks up to Alurich.

CHARLES

Welcome

ALURICH

Hello

CHARLES

How are you doing my friend?

ALURICH

Not too good. My wife, where do they keep the
women here?

CHARLES

You married?

ALURICH

Yeah, we were brought here this morning and
separated

CHARLES

I'm sorry, let me introduce myself. Charles
Anderson

ALURICH

Alurich Korall

CHARLES

As you can see the living conditions aren't all
that. The women are kept in a different section.
So what do you do?

ALURICH

I'm a welder

CHARLES

Oh, you're a welder; you'll be working with me.
Here, these are the guys

There are a group of five men sitting on the floor playing cards.

CHARLES (CONT'D)

This is Paul, Alex, Nathaniel, Herman and Stan.
Guys, this is Alurich. He's a welder

ALL

Hey

ALURICH

Hello, how are you men?

NATHANIEL

Could be better, I'm down ten toothpicks.

ALURICH

Toothpicks, why not blankets or pillows?

PAUL

Believe me; I lost my toenail clipper last night.

There is an old dusty wooden piano by the barrack wall.

ALURICH

Who's piano?

CHARLES

That piano has been here since I came. I don't
know whose it is

Alurich takes a seat in front of the piano.

                    ALURICH

Does anybody play?

                    CHARLES

No

Alurich taps a few keys.

                    ALURICH

This piano is out of tune

Alurich begins tuning the piano.

EXT. SECTION A - NIGHT

                    JANSDALTER

So how long have you been in the military?

                    PENDENGROB

Long enough to know what it is like to kill a
man

                    JANSDALTER

And how long is that?

                    PENDENGROB

I started out in the infantry just like any other
slave. Then I moved up to part-time killer.
Now I'm a full-time killer

                    JANSDALTER

What do you mean part-time killer?

                    PENDENGROB

I mean I used to be a sniper and kill people

only part of the time. Now I am a full-time life
ender

                    JANSDALTER
Why are you always drinking?

                    PENDENGROB
Because it's good

Pendengrob offers Jansdalter a drink.

                    JANSDALTER
No, I don't drink

                    PENDENGROB
Haha, he doesn't drink. You will learn boy

                    JANSDALTER
So what are we doing?

                    PENDENGROB
We are watching

Pendengrob grabs a seat by barrack one and takes a magazine out of
his jacket. He gulps a swig of whiskey.

                PENDENGROB (CONT'D)
This is how you watch

                    JANSDALTER
It sounds like a piano

                    PENDENGROB
Oh, you hear that too? I thought it was me. La
dee da dee da.

No, listen, it's coming from inside

INT. SECTION A, BARRACK ONE - NIGHT

Pendengrob and Jansdalter open the door as Alurich finishes playing the piano.

CHARLES

That was amazing. Your playing is immaculate man. Where did you learn to play like that?

PENDENGROB

That was good

Everyone exerts their attention towards the two soldiers.

ALURICH

Oh, I'm sorry

PENDENGROB

No, no, it's ok. You see, that piano was sent here to Snyder by somebody and nobody even touches it. I was going to use the damn thing for firewood, but he wouldn't let me. Behave! I'll be back...maybe

Jansdalter and Pendengrob exit.

ALURICH

Who were they?

CHARLES

The man talking was Sig Pendengrob. I don't think I've seen him sober for one minute since I've been here

ALURICH

So the officers go around drunk.

CHARLES

Only Pendengrob, a guard watches the barrack
at all times.

ALURICH

That makes it impossible to escape

CHARLES

There are many things that make it impossible
to escape. That is one of them

ALURICH

Is there any way to find out if my wife is still
alive?

CHARLES

The two sides never communicate with each
other. I don't know. Listen, you have had a
long day. It's best if you get good nights sleep.
Tomorrow will be a long day too

ALURICH

Where should I...

CHARLES

It looks like you're on the floor tonight buddy.
All of the bunks are taken. First come, first get
around here

ALURICH

Right

CHARLES

Well, I will see you in the morning, good night
buddy

Alurich lies down on the floor and falls asleep.

INT. SECTION B, BARRACK TWO - NIGHT

Freya is sitting on the floor propped up against a wooden bunker of
beds. A middle aged woman comes up behind her.

BETH

You seem troubled dear

Freya turns around.

FREYA

I thought you might have been dead!

BETH

No, I didn't know about you either

FREYA

They came this morning and, and they
completely trashed our place. They took
everything we had...

BETH

Calm down dear

FREYA

Where were you?

BETH

We were checking on our neighbors. We got

there, everyone was gone and that's when we
were met by...

FREYA

Yes, go on

BETH

They killed your father

FREYA

What?

Both women begin to cry. A woman lying in the bunk behind them
interrupts.

WOMAN

Hey, would you two keep it down. I'm trying to
sleep here

Beth and Freya walk over to an open corner.

BETH

We need to stay calm, just have faith for being
alive. How is Alurich?

FREYA

I don't know mom. I don't know anything!

BETH

Ok, did they take Alurich to a section?

FREYA

Yeah

BETH

Do you know which one?

FREYA

I only thought there were two

BETH

No, there are three. Isn't that what you said
Elise?

A beautiful young woman named Elise sits across from them.

ELISE

Yeah, there's three sections

FREYA

Well, if the first section is for the men and the
second is for the women. What is the third one
for?

ELISE

Come with me

The three women walk outside.

EXT. SECTION B, BARRACK TWO - NIGHT

Elise points at the smoking chimney in the distance.

ELISE

The fire is the funeral

INT. SECTION B, BARRACK TWO - NIGHT

The three women walk back into the crowded barrack.

FREYA

They burn the damn bodies? Are you kidding
me?

BETH

If we stay strong I doubt we will be sent there

FREYA

I'm going to be sick. I feel so...I'm going to be sick. Oh no...

ELISE

Don't throw up on me

BETH

You need to sit down dear

EXT. SECTION B - NIGHT

PENDENGROB

That guy played well

JANSDALTER

Yes, he won't get in trouble?

PENDENGROB

It's possible. Some of the guards care, some don't, I don't

JANSDALTER

If the officers don't care then how do you keep this camp running?

PENDENGROB

Ha! You will find out kid. This is camp B, where the women are

JANSDALTER

Yes, I know

PENDENGROB

Your duty for the next two weeks will be watch duty over barrack two. You remember how I told you to watch?

JANSDALTER

Yeah

PENDENGROB

Well, you do the same here. You sit, and you watch

INT. SECTION B, BARRACK TWO - NIGHT

ELISE

You two make me laugh. We're all gonna die, you know it, I know it

BETH

Be quiet Elise

FREYA

I'm worried about Alurich

ELISE

He's probably dead

BETH

Quiet Elise!

ELISE

Only if he's lucky

Pendengrob and Jansdalter enter the barrack.

PENDENGROB

It is your job to keep an eye on these women.
This is where they stay, this is what they do.
Attention everyone, this is Jansbralter, he will be
watching you...outside

JANSDALTER

My name is Jansdalter, not bralter

PENDENGROB

Like I said, this is Jansbralter, he has a gun.
(Drunk Shouting) Do you hear that!?

All of the women ignore Pendengrob. The two soldiers exit the
barrack.

EXT. SECTION B, BARRACK TWO - NIGHT

JANSDALTER

You know, I don't have a gun. Well, I do but
I've never used it

PENDENGROB

You won't need to, Snyder put you on watch
because you don't know what the hell is going
on. Just sit in your chair and relax. There are
magazines. Make sure you stay awake

Pendengrob leaves and Jansdalter grabs a magazine. He leans back
into the chair and the legs break as he hits the floor.

INT. AUDITORIUM - DAY

A crowd of soldiers sit in aligned chairs and listen to Snyder give his
speech. A curtain covers the stage.

SNYDER

As all of you know we are responsible for
running this camp properly with no question of
moral. As the commandant of this camp I am
here to inform you of your duties. I have been
a member of the Black Coats for the past fifteen
years of my life. I am now reaching middle-age
and expect this establishment to be ran the way
I say. I do not have the time or patience for
nonsense. I know that some of you might not
support the cause, or may decide to retaliate and
do unacceptable work.

Snyder pulls the curtain from the stage and reveals Haas hanging by
the neck from rope in full uniform, dead.

SNYDER (CONT'D)

Many of you men knew this man by the name
of Haas. Now you know him as the former
Haas. It is unfortunate that his life had to be
taken, but let him stand as an example to you all
of the consequences that you may face for not
meeting my expectations. It is the cause that is
important, remember that. We must all work
together to reach the goals at hand, and his work
ethic was absolutely intolerable. I am a highly
respected member of this force and it would be
greatly unwise for any of you to plot against me,
but I assure that if you men reach credibility
that all of you will be rewarded graciously. Now
that all of us are acquainted with one another
I can assure you complete prominence. Does
anybody have any questions?

Nobody says a word.

SNYDER (CONT'D)

Does anybody not know what they are supposed to be doing?

Nobody says a word.

SNYDER (CONT'D)

Then do it.

Every soldier in the auditorium scurries out of their chairs.

SNYDER (CONT'D)

I will let him hang here for a weeks time to give you men recollection. Look to him as a martyr for our motivation

INT. SECTION A, BARRACK SIX - DAY

The prisoners are welding war supplies and other necessities.

ALURICH

You do very nice work

CHARLES
(Pulling his mask up)
What?

ALURICH

I said you do very nice work.

CHARLES

Thanks buddy

ALURICH

Perhaps you could teach me a few things.

CHARLES

Oh, you're not going to learn anything from me

ALURICH

I'm looking for something to do.

CHARLES

You see those sprockets over there; they need to be welded to the metal flanges sitting on that table

ALURICH

Oh, ok, thanks

Alurich walks over to the table and attempts to weld the pieces, but doesn't know how to light the torch.

ALURICH (CONT'D)

How do you use that torch?

CHARLES

What are you talkin' about man?

ALURICH

I've never seen that model before.

CHARLES

They only make one model

It's clear that Alurich doesn't have any idea what he's doing.

CHARLES (CONT'D)

Come over here, I will show you. First, you

take the torch and you light it, see. Place the
metal on the table, hold it steady, make sure
not to get too close to the flange or you'll burn
right through the sprocket. There, done. I can't
believe you've never used a torch like this. What
kind of welder are you anyways?

ALURICH

I've never welded anything before

CHARLES

What? How did you make it here, you'd be
killed

ALURICH

That's why I wrote out a fake

CHARLES

A fake? How did you do that? They know the
fakes

ALURICH

A counterfeiter, a friend of mine who's now dead
disguised one. He was a master at plagiarism
and created a false identity for me

CHARLES

Why are you telling me this? You know, there
are spies wandering these barracks posing as you
and me

ALURICH

You are the only friend I have here. I need your
help

CHARLES

You realize you're putting all of our lives at risk
here at an attempt to save yourself

ALURICH

I know

CHARLES

I will teach you everything. We have a fixed
amount everyday so make sure you keep your
stock up. Start with the handles, they're simple
enough. Here, follow me outside

EXT. SECTION A, BARRACK SIX - DAY

Alurich and Charles walk outside and duck next to a window.

CHARLES
(Taking out a map)
Do you remember how you were asking about
your wife?

ALURICH

Yeah, what is that?

CHARLES

It is a map

ALURICH

A map?

CHARLES

Shhh!! When this camp was built they
originally had an underground tunnel that
connected sections A and B together. Here is
the layout. The tunnel still exists. When I first

arrived here I would meet my wife there during
the night

ALURICH

So you're saying there is a chance I can see Freya

CHARLES

Not actually see her. They built a brick wall to
serve as a blockade. The tunnel was originally
going to be used for transporting goods

ALURICH

Is it safe?

CHARLES

No, you must sneak down there during the
night. My wife and I would meet every Tuesday
and Friday. You must follow the creek behind
our barrack

ALURICH

There's barbed wire blocking that

CHARLES

Crawl under it, the creek will take you to a
passage underground. Write your wife a letter;
sew it into your clothing. If she is alive she will
be on laundry, which is where the women start

ALURICH

Do you still meet with your wife?

CHARLES

No

ALURICH

Why did you stop?

CHARLES

I went down to the tunnel on a Friday night, and she wasn't there. I've never heard from her since

EXT. CAMP HEADQUARTERS ROOF - DAY

Five soldiers dressed in black uniforms walk up to the roof.

SNYDER

Jansdalter, today is a special day for you sir

SHATZI

I want to shoot!

PENDENGROB

You couldn't kill a man standing five feet from you

SHATZI

And I suppose you could do better?

PENDENGROB

I killed over 200 men in one sitting during the war

SHATZI

Which war?

PENDENGROB

I don't remember

SHATZI

I don't believe you

SNYDER

It's true. Corporal Larry Pendengrob was one of the military's finest snipers

SHATZI

Even if it is true that was then. Look at him, now he's so drunk he can't even walk straight

HERNANDEZ

Shatzi does have a point Larry

PENDENGROB

I shoot better when I'm drunk. Pick an object

SHATZI

Anyone?

PENDENGROB

Object, person, it doesn't matter

Shatzi finds Alurich standing all alone 300 feet away.

SHATZI

There, him

PENDENGROB
(Pointing to Alurich)

Him?

SHATZI

Yes, him, kill him

PENDENGROB

That's too easy. We'll leave him for the boy.
Pick something else

Shatzi searches the camp and finds Freya sitting on the barrack steps talking to a fellow prisoner.

SHATZI

Her

PENDENGROB

The woman sitting on the steps?

SHATZI

Yes, shoot her

Pendengrob fires a shot at Freya. He misses and the bullet hits the doorknob. Freya and the other woman jump up in shock.

SHATZI (CONT'D)

He missed! I told you he'd miss

HERNANDEZ
(Lowering the binoculars)
It would have been good if he had been aiming
for the doorknob

PENDENGROB

Let me try again

SHATZI

No second chances, it's my turn

PENDENGROB

I'm going to shoot the coffee mug

SHATZI

What coffee mug?

PENDENGROB

The mug in that officer's hand

SHATZI

What?! You can't shoot at him, he's an officer

PENDENGROB

I'm not going to shoot him. I'm going to shoot
his coffee mug. I won't miss this time

SHATZI

That's what you said last time. Colonel Snyder
sir! I request that you order Corporal Larry
Pendengrob to put down his weapon at once!
He is a threat to endanger the life of a fellow
officer!

SNYDER

He won't miss

Pendengrob fires a shot at an officer sitting on the steps in Section A.
The mug shatters as the officer takes a drink. Coffee spills all over his
newspaper.

HERNANDEZ

That's amazing, your accuracy is incredible

PENDENGROB

I know

SNYDER

It's time for the boy to try

PENDENGROB

Here, I'll hold your ice cream

Pendengrob takes Jansdalter's ice cream cone and gives him the rifle.

PENDENGROB (CONT'D)

Let's aim for that man we were going to shoot
before

Pendengrob holds the gun with Jansdalter and places his hand on top
of Jansdalter's.

PENDENGROB (CONT'D)

You look through the eyepiece and concentrate
on him, mimicking his every move. Picture him
as if he weren't even alive. Position the lines
with the target; you're a part of him now. You
breathe with him, you move with him, he will
know when it is his time and so will you. When
he does, he will accept you as his taker. It is
time, kill him now.

Jansdalter shakes fiercely. He fires a shot at Alurich and misses,
hitting the ground near his feet.

PENDENGROB (CONT'D)

It's ok. The first time is difficult for everyone.
Perhaps he was bad luck, we'll pick someone
different.

SNYDER

No, we don't have time. We need to report back
to duty.

Snyder, Hernandez, and Shatzi leave the roof. Pendengrob ate over
half of Jansdalter's ice cream cone. He gives the half eaten cone back
to Jansdalter.

INT. SECTION B, BARRACK FIVE - DAY

Freya is standing in front of a laundry basket sorting through clothes. Several other women are on laundry duty. Freya finds a letter inside of a prisoner's uniform. She reads the letter and places it inside her pocket.

EXT. SECTION B, BARRACK FIVE - SUNSET

The women have been dismissed from work. Freya runs out of the barrack and into barrack two.

INT. SECTION B, BARRACK TWO - SUNSET

Freya runs towards Elise and Beth.

                    FREYA
               (Out of breath)
        Look! I got a letter from Alurich

                    BETH
        What!? Let me see, what does it say?

                    FREYA
        He says there's a passage that connects both of
        the sections. He wants me to meet him there

                    BETH
        This is great Freya, but how can you be sure this
        is safe?

                    ELISE
        She's right; guards will purposely slip notes into
        the laundry

FREYA

It's in his handwriting. He writes dear Freya,
I am alive. I'm working as a welder. I am
not very good at it, but haven't been caught
yet. How are you? Good I hope. There is an
underground passage that connects both of the
sections together. I will be there this Friday at
thirteen night. I have drawn a map on the back
of this letter that shows you how to get there. It
should be quite easy. I hope to see you there,
with love, Alurich. The map shows that the
passage is located behind our barrack next to the
creek

BETH

I know this is important to you dear, but it
sounds risky. We don't want anything bad to
happen

FREYA

I'm willing to take that chance. If I don't see
him I'll just wait here and nothing will happen.
I want out of this place, don't you?

BETH

We all do dear

ELISE

Friday night Beth and I will keep a watch for
you. Plan on taking no longer than an hour
before anyone notices you're gone, ok?

FREYA

Ok

ELISE

Good

INT. BREAK ROOM - SUNSET

Snyder, Hernandez, Pendengrob, Shatzi, and Jansdalter are standing inside the break room. A male prisoner is on his knees motionless in front of them.

SNYDER

We are going to try this one more time. Shatzi, the gun

Shatzi hands Snyder his pistol and Snyder offers it to Jansdalter.

SNYDER (CONT'D)

Put the gun to his head

Jansdalter takes the gun from Snyder and puts it to the side of the prisoner's head. The prisoner doesn't have a reaction.

SNYDER (CONT'D)

Now pull the trigger and release

Jansdalter shakes terribly and cannot kill the man. Snyder puts his pistol to the side of Jansdalter's head.

SNYDER (CONT'D)

Kill him

Jansdalter kills the prisoner.

SNYDER (CONT'D)

Good, now take a picture of him

Jansdalter takes a picture of the dead prisoner.

SNYDER (CONT'D)

Everyone report to duty

Pendengrob and Shatzi exit the break room.

SNYDER (CONT'D)

Jansdalter, I want you to remove the body and
get this mess cleaned up.

HERNANDEZ

I'll help you

SNYDER

No, he will do it himself

Jansdalter begins dragging the body out of the break room.

SNYDER (CONT'D)

You are beginning to make big strides Officer
Jansdalter. You came and you didn't even know
how to shoot a gun, now you have your first kill

Shatzi enters the break room.

SHATZI

Colonel Snyder sir, Sergeant Shatzi reporting!

Shatzi salutes Snyder as an older man dressed in a suit enters the
room behind him. Dr. Krouse carries a briefcase and is wearing
glasses.

SNYDER

Hello sir

KROUSE

I am Dr. Haewood Krouse

                        SNYDER

        Dr. Krouse, would you like a drink sir?

                        KROUSE

        No, I am quite fine, thank you

Krouse takes out a book of papers from his briefcase and hands them
to Snyder.

                    KROUSE (CONT'D)

        I have come here to give you these. They are
        orders sent down from the man. I suggest you
        follow them. The outlines of your duties are
        explained in the packet. Your job is to take a
        man, any man, and perform the experiments
        written in the text

                        SNYDER

        Can you give me an approximation of your
        return Doctor?

                        KROUSE

        I will visit the camp periodically to collect
        your data. Until then, concentrate on the task.
        Good day sir

Dr. Krouse exits the room.

EXT. SECTION B, BARRACK TWO - NIGHT

Freya sneaks out of the back window. Elise and Beth keep a watch
out for her. Pendengrob is passed out in a chair in front of barrack
two with a bottle of rum and a magazine in his lap. Freya rolls under
the barbed wire fence behind the barrack and down a hill into a ditch
in front of a creek. She crawls on her knees to the tunnel and avoids
the search light.

                        - 40 -

INT. TUNNEL - NIGHT

Freya walks through the tunnel and up to a brick wall.

FREYA

Alurich!

ALURICH

Freya!

Alurich and Freya reach the brick wall that divides them simultaneously, each on one side of the wall.

FREYA

Are you ok?

ALURICH

Yeah, how are you?

FREYA

I'm ok, just tired and hungry

ALURICH

Did you have any trouble making it out?

FREYA

No, I made it out fine, how about you?

ALURICH

I made it out fine

FREYA

My mom is in the same barrack I am. Her and this girl named Elise made a lookout for me

ALURICH

How is your mother?

FREYA

Like the rest of us. I heard about your friend.
That's good you have someone helping you out

ALURICH

Yeah, I wouldn't be able to make it without him.
Listen, we need to figure out a way to get out of
here

FREYA

I know, got any ideas because I've thought of it a
lot and haven't come up with anything

ALURICH

No, I've been talking to Charles. It seems the
only way out of here would be revolt, but that
would ultimately mean death

FREYA

Maybe we can wait it out

ALURICH

I'll keep my ears out for anything. If I think it
will work then I'll let you know

FREYA

I don't want to go back

ALURICH

We can sit down here all night, but we'll
eventually have to go back for food, and when
we do we'll be caught. It's ok if we come down

here twice a week, but we have to keep the time short

FREYA

I know

ALURICH

It's been a long day. We should be getting back

FREYA

I'll be back here Tuesday night, plan on it

ALURICH

So will I…I love you

FREYA

Yeah…

ALURICH

What?

FREYA

I don't know. I'm messed up right now

ALURICH

Yeah…we all are. Be careful

FREYA

I will

ALURICH

I'm leaving now

FREYA

I'll see you. Be careful, I love you

ALURICH

Goodbye. Stay strong

Alurich and Freya exit the tunnel.

EXT. SECTION A - DAY

Shatzi, Pendengrob, Snyder, and Jansdalter walk in a line side by side. Shatzi has a mean snarl on his face and carries his assault rifle. Pendengrob is intoxicated and carries a bottle of gin. Snyder is emotionless and carries his pocket watch on his belt. Jansdalter is depressed and has his camera strapped around his neck. This is a slow motion close-up shot of each soldier that's purpose reveals characterization.

INT. SECTION A, BARRACK SIX - DAY

Snyder enters the barrack. Three soldiers follow his path. Alurich and Charles are welding inside the barrack.

SNYDER

Those are nice hinges you are making

ALURICH

Thank you

SNYDER

Are these the hinges you have made today?

ALURICH

Yes

SNYDER

That's not many hinges, and this hinge has a bad
weld. Are you aware of this?

ALURICH

Yes, I was nervous

SNYDER

Why were you nervous?

ALURICH

Because you're standing behind me

Snyder dumps the box of hinges onto the table.

SNYDER

All of these hinges have been welded incorrectly.
Why would a man who is an expert welder,
weld so poorly, and so slow?

Alurich does not answer.

SNYDER (CONT'D)

Do you know what I think we have? I think we
have a liar gentlemen. Let's show what we do
with liars

Snyder and the three officers escort Alurich out of the barrack.

INT. ROOM THIRTEEN - DAY

Snyder, Hernandez and the three officers escort Alurich into the
room.

SNYDER

Let's get this started. Tie him up

The three officers tie Alurich to the wall with his back turned.

SNYDER (CONT'D)

Put this on him

Snyder hands an officer a black blindfold. The officer ties the blindfold around Alurich's face and over his eyes.

SNYDER (CONT'D)

Remove his shirt

Two officers remove Alurich's shirt. Snyder rings a bell and Hernandez plugs a chain saw into an outlet. He places the chain saw next to Alurich's face for a good thirteen seconds and then takes it away. Alurich is shaking fiercely. An officer walks over to Alurich with a white sack. He pulls a snake out of the sack and places it around Alurich's neck.

SNYDER (CONT'D)

Get the glass case

An officer brings a glass case filled with scorpions over to Alurich and places the scorpions onto his body.

ALURICH

What the hell are you doing to me?

HERNANDEZ

Do you think that's enough?

SNYDER

The five minutes are not complete

The snake and scorpions continue to squirm.

SNYDER (CONT'D)

That is enough for today

The officers remove the snake and scorpions from Alurich's skin and untie him from the wall. They escort him from the room and everyone exits.

INT. UNDERGROUND CELL - DAY

The officers take Alurich to a pitch black underground cell. An officer removes his blindfold once they reach the cell. There are two iron rings connected to a concrete wall. The floor below the rings is covered with shattered glass. Snyder shines a flashlight on the glass.

SNYDER

Do you know what this is? It is broken glass

The officers escort Alurich to the wall and tie him to the iron rings above the shattered glass with chains. All of the officers walk up the stairs and exit the cell.

EXT. SECTION B - DAY

Freya, Beth, and Elise wait outside in a food line. There are four separate lines. A male cook stands in front of the table with a pot of soup, bowls, and loafs of bread.

ELISE

I'm starving; I don't know how long they can make us wait for this

The three women move forward in line.

ELISE (CONT'D)

Oh, oh, we're moving, we're moving

The three women reach the table and the cook gives them each a bowl of soup, cup of water, and slice of bread. They walk over to a bare area and take a seat on the ground. The women begin to eat their meal together.

ELISE (CONT'D)

I swear I'd sleep with an officer here just for a piece of cake. Oh, I would love a piece of chocolate cake right now

FREYA

Hey, you gotta do what you gotta do. This isn't food; I don't care what anyone says this isn't food.

BETH

How is Alurich doing?

FREYA

He's alright, its hard being away from him

BETH

So do you plan on seeing him again?

FREYA

Tomorrow night

BETH

Do you need us to keep a lookout again?

FREYA

I made it out pretty easily the last time. I don't think it's necessary. I don't want either of you to get killed over me

ELISE

Yeah, I agree, it's best if we just stay out of this. I'm finished

FREYA

If that drunken slob is still watching our barrack
I won't have any problems

BETH

Just promise me you'll be careful

FREYA

Of course mother

The cook blows his whistle and all of the women run to the table and
quickly empty their trash into a waste basket.

COOK

Make it fast! Make it fast ladies

EXT. CAMP ENTRY - DAY

Flanigan, Hernandez, and Pendengrob are by the train.

FLANIGAN

I can't believe we have to attach these hitches

HERNANDEZ

Snyder gave us orders bro

FLANIGAN

Hey, I haven't slept for two days here. I can't
sleep at night thinking about what I do during
the day. I have a headache

HERNANDEZ

Listen, after we attach these trailers you take a
nap

FLANIGAN

Fine

PENDENGROB

Here, you and Hernandez go push the trailer
and I'll connect it

FLANIGAN

Why can't you push it?

PENDENGROB

That's what I said, I'll push it and you connect...

FLANIGAN

(Interrupting)
Yeah yeah yeah

Pendengrob and Hernandez push the trailer forward. Flanigan is
standing asleep next to the train. A loud scream is heard.

FLANIGAN (CONT'D)

Ahhh!

Pendengrob and Hernandez walk back over to Flanigan.

FLANIGAN (CONT'D)

I'm stuck! I'm stuck! You son-of-a...

PENDENGROB

Go get Snyder

Hernandez takes off towards the camp.

PENDENGROB (CONT'D)

Where are you stuck at?

FLANIGAN

(Screaming) I can't believe you did this to me!

PENDENGROB

Grab on to me and I'll pull you out

FLANIGAN

What?! No! I can't move! We're going to have
to derail the hitch and move the trailer back

PENDENGROB

I'm not strong enough to do that

FLANIGAN

I know that!

PENDENGROB

(Offering his whiskey)
Here, calm down, Peter went to get Snyder. You
want something to drink?

FLANIGAN

(Throwing the bottle down)
What?! No! Help me! Please God help me!

Snyder and Hernandez arrive.

SNYDER

What is going on here?

FLANIGAN

I'm stuck!

PENDENGROB

Hernandez and I were pushing the trailer towards the train and we crushed this guy. Now he's stuck

FLANIGAN

I can't feel my legs

SNYDER

You're numb, you're cold as well

HERNANDEZ

Let's unlatch the hitch

SNYDER

We cannot do that

HERNANDEZ

What? Why not?

SNYDER

Because it's the only thing keeping him alive; if we unlatch the hitch his organs will collapse and he'll die instantly. I've seen this

FLANIGAN

This has happened before?! You've gotta be kidding me! I can't even feel anything

SNYDER

Circulation is being cut off. You're in shock. The only thing holding your internal organs together is pressure from the hitch

FLANIGAN

No, no, call a doctor, this is crazy, get an
ambulance

SNYDER

I'm afraid the nearest doctor is miles away.
There's nothing a medic could do, they would
tell you the same thing I have

FLANIGAN

Is there anything we can do? I'm losing feeling

PENDENGROB

His face is turning blue

HERNANDEZ

His lips are swollen, he's shaking

SNYDER

He is going to die. Keep the latch hooked for as
long as you want. Call Officer Flanigan's family.
Tell them to come to Nordfels at once. Their
son is dying

FLANIGAN

I didn't want anything to do with this camp
or stupid private under the table murder crap.
Did you hear that? This is all crooked! All of
it! I'm too young to die. I had a wife! A hot
wife! She's pregnant! So screw you! Where's
my money?!

PENDENGROB

What money?

FLANIGAN

(Shouting) I was promised money! I haven't
seen any money!

PENDENGROB

You got paid?

FLANIGAN

Screw you Larry!

SNYDER

Very good, I will have someone bring you
blankets for warmth. You don't need to freeze
to death. Until then, move your body as little
as possible. Your family will be contacted, but
there is no guarantee they will be here before the
time of your departure. This train will leave the
premises no later than five this afternoon. There
is a new shipment coming in tomorrow. Your
work here has been much appreciated Officer
Flanigan, congratulations. We must get back to
duty now

Snyder, Hernandez, and Pendengrob walk away and enter the camp.

INT. SECTION B, BARRACK TWO - NIGHT

Elise, Beth, and Freya are in the barrack with several other women.
Elise and Beth are looking out the window at Pendengrob, who is
passed out in a chair in front of barrack two with a bottle of rum and
a magazine. They motion for Freya to sneak out the back window,
and she does.

INT. TUNNEL - NIGHT

Freya walks up to the brick wall.

FREYA

Alurich! Can you hear me?

There is no response.

FREYA (CONT'D)
(Shouting)

Alurich!

There is no response. Freya leaves the tunnel.

INT. ROOM THIRTEEN - DAY

Snyder, Hernandez, and two other officers are in the room. Alurich
is blindfolded and tied to the wall with his back against everyone.
Snyder rings a bell that sits on the nearby table.

ALURICH

It is time to begin

Burns and cut wounds cover Alurich's body. An officer begins slicing
his forearms and chest with a knife. Alurich bleeds.

HERNANDEZ

We are slicing his skin like butter, but he's not
reacting

Snyder looks puzzled. A second officer burns Alurich's back with a
steaming hot iron. Alurich doesn't have a reaction.

HERNANDEZ (CONT'D)

Is he dead?

SNYDER

That is enough for today. Take him down

Hernandez and the other two officers untie Alurich and he falls back into their arms.

EXT. SECTION B - NIGHT

Pendengrob and Jansdalter walk through Section B.

                    PENDENGROB
          So, are you ready?

                    JANSDALTER
          Ready for what?

                    PENDENGROB
                    (Laughing)
          Ready to find a woman

                    JANSDALTER
          Oh, yes sir

                    PENDENGROB
          Good, so tell me Jansbralter, what kind of
          women do you like?

                    JANSDALTER
          Oh, any kind I guess

                    PENDENGROB
          You will have a very wide range

They reach the first three barracks.

                    PENDENGROB (CONT'D)
          Well Mr. Jansbralter, you pick which barrack

                          JANSDALTER

    That one

                          PENDENGROB

    Ah, barrack two, nice choice, many nice women
    in number two, after you

INT. SECTION B, BARRACK TWO - NIGHT

The barrack is crowded with women. Freya, Beth, and Elise sit by
each other on the floor.

                            BETH

    So, did you see Alurich last night? How is he
    doing?

                           FREYA

    He wasn't there

Pendengrob and Jansdalter enter the barrack and stand in front of the
door.

                         PENDENGROB
                         (Whispering)
    So, which one do you want?

                         JANSDALTER
                         (Whispering)
    I don't know

                         PENDENGROB

    It's just like a whore house isn't it? It's tough to
    choose

Jansdalter is silent. He gazes around the room and his eyes suddenly
meet with Freya's.

                    JANSDALTER
                    (Whispering)
          Her

                    PENDENGROB
          Miss, you need to come with us.

Freya points to herself.

                    PENDENGROB (CONT'D)
          Yes, you. Come with us please

Freya stands up and exits the barrack with Pendengrob and Jansdalter.

EXT. SECTION B, BARRACK TWO - NIGHT

Pendengrob, Jasndalter, and Freya walk from barrack two to barrack
eight. Pendengrob takes Jansdalter aside.

                    PENDENGROB
                    (Whispering)
          Take her with you inside this barrack. I'll keep
          a watch out for you. Have fun

                    JANSDALTER
          Miss, would you mind stepping inside please?

Freya and Jansdalter enter the barrack.

INT. SECTION B, BARRACK EIGHT - NIGHT

Freya and Jansdalter walk to the center of the room.

                    JANSDALTER
          Remove your clothing please

FREYA

What?

JANSDALTER

I need you to remove your clothing

FREYA

Why?

JANSDALTER

I have brought you in here because I need to
have sex with you

FREYA
(Laughing)

What? I'm a married woman

JANSDALTER

That doesn't matter. Who is your husband?

FREYA

I can't tell you that, unless you're willing to help
me

JANSDALTER

With what?

FREYA

How do I know I can trust you? I mean what
if I tell you his name and you try to kill him
or something because you like me? How do I
know you won't try to kill me?

JANSDALTER

I don't even know your name

- 59 -

FREYA

Freya

JANSDALTER

Hello Freya, I am Officer Cedric Jansdalter.
What do you need help with?

FREYA

I don't know if my husband is alive or not. He
is being kept here at this camp

JANSDALTER

What is his name?

FREYA

Alurich Korall, can you help me? I would really
appreciate it

JANSDALTER

I will find out if your husband is alive or not

FREYA

Will you? That would be so nice

JANSDALTER

Don't tell anyone, how old are you?

FREYA

Twenty-three, what about you?

JANSDALTER

Seventeen

FREYA

That's really young to be in the military

JANSDALTER

I was drafted

FREYA

The draft is over. It's been over

JANSDALTER

I know. So are we going to do it or not?

FREYA

What?! No! Wait a minute, if the draft is over,
and you're only seventeen, then what are you
doing here?

JANSDALTER

I'm a photographer. I heard of a job for the
military here for good pay. I graduated early
and they took me in. This is not what I
expected. Now, I'm sort of stuck. I would be
killed like any of us

FREYA

All of this is illegal

JANSDALTER

There is an officer waiting outside this barrack
for me and he insists that I sleep with one of the
women here or he won't leave me alone

FREYA

Why is he so interested in your sexuality? Is he
gay?

JANSDALTER

No, just perverted

FREYA

No, wait, I have a better idea. Listen to this

Freya starts shouting out fake orgasms.

JANSDALTER

What are you doing?

Freya continues to shout out in ecstasy.

EXT. SECTION B, BARRACK EIGHT - NIGHT

Pendengrob is standing by the door and overhears the loud orgasms.
He places his ear against the door.

FREYA

Oh Yes! Cedric! You make me feel so good!
Thank you! Thank you so much!

Pendengrob is both shocked and aroused by what he hears.

INT. SECTION B, BARRACK EIGHT - NIGHT

Freya finally ends her orgasmic rampage.

FREYA

How was that?

JANSDALTER

Loud

FREYA

I hope he heard me

EXT. SECTION B, BARRACK EIGHT - NIGHT

Freya and Jansdalter exit the barrack. Pendengrob is standing next to the door.

> FREYA
>
> That was great

She kisses Jansdalter on his nose and walks away. Pendengrob is speechless. He stares at Jansdalter.

> JANSDALTER
>
> What?

Pendengrob starts laughing hysterically and walks away.

INT. ROOM THIRTEEN - DAY

Snyder, Dr. Krouse, Alurich, Jansdalter, Hernandez, and an unknown soldier are in the room. Alurich is blindfolded and tied against the wall with his back turned to the men. The unknown soldier gives Alurich repetitive slashes with the whip and Alurich doesn't have a reaction. Snyder takes the whip out of the soldier's hand and gives Alurich an incredibly vicious blow to the back.

> ALURICH
>
> Is that all you have?

Snyder is dumbfounded. He releases three violent blows.

> ALURICH (CONT'D)
>
> I figured a man of your esteem would have more
> to offer, how weak

> SNYDER
>
> Who are you?

ALURICH

I do not know

SNYDER

How could you not know who you are?

ALURICH

I do not know

SNYDER

Take him down

Hernandez and Jansdalter untie Alurich from the wall.

ALURICH

My name is Alurich Korall

Snyder stops once he hears Alurich speak, and then exits the room with Dr. Krouse.

INT. SNYDER'S OFFICE - DAY

Snyder and Dr. Krouse take a seat at the desk.

SNYDER

I'm moments away from killing him

KROUSE
(Laughing)
You sound aggravated Colonel

SNYDER

I don't understand. It's like beating on a piece
of meat. He has no reactions, emotions. It
seems the more we torture him the less poignant
he becomes

KROUSE

Then this experiment has proven itself successful

SNYDER

You still haven't told me the point behind all of
this

KROUSE

Oh it's quite simple really, manipulation, control

SNYDER

It seems the despot must be afraid of revolt

KROUSE

We haven't won the war yet

SNYDER

They say we have, if you want to call it that, but
how can you win a war that isn't your own?

KROUSE

I'm surprised by your skepticism Colonel; you've
been nothing but loyal up to this point

SNYDER

It's not a question of loyalty. I believe in
tyranny, but also freedom. The two can coexist

KROUSE

Can they?

SNYDER

They can if there is equilibrium

KROUSE

How can there be equilibrium under
competition?

SNYDER

Control

KROUSE

How can there be control over freedom?

SNYDER

Justice

KROUSE

How can there be justice when diplomacy is
dead?

SNYDER

You sound like the skeptic Doctor

KROUSE

I never said I wasn't

SNYDER

So why are we doing this?

KROUSE

The government seems to be terrified of anarchy
if it is proven a success

SNYDER

Murder and greed is not the answer

KROUSE
(Laughing)
Have you spoken about this to the despot?

SNYDER

I would be the next one tied up to the wall, but I am only one, tyranny can be successful under small majority, but millions?

KROUSE

I must disagree; I believe the opposite, propaganda

SNYDER

Through what?

KROUSE

Freedom of speech

SNYDER

Manipulation

KROUSE

Yes

SNYDER

So I suppose you condition a person to pain through habit and any manipulation is possible.

KROUSE

We're just toughening him up. You're catching on colonel. There can be complete control through two things: Habit and belief. Chain the public to falsehood while the government has complete dominance over the world

SNYDER

So you're saying there isn't any difference between capitalism and communism. I must disagree.

Tyranny has a bad reputation in a class society,
it won't work. Families must stay close for
the caste to prevail, keep the wealth in a small
majority to rule

KROUSE

The self gratifying majority; let those who
choose to fish, they won't know that there aren't
any fish in the sea

SNYDER

Totalitarian conservatism, so we beat a man into
submission, so much that he gives up on hope,
and the citizens as well, and a few may slip
between the cracks and benefit. So tell me this
Doctor, what happens when the beast becomes
too powerful for its creator?

KROUSE

Anarchy, eventually the levee breaks, it always
breaks. It is inevitable

SNYDER

It is in a land of emptiness and confusion. A
lack of love

KROUSE

Do you believe love can exist in an unhealthy
environment?

SNYDER

If the person is strong enough to separate
the two; only hope can exist in such an
environment. This will not work. All people
are not fools sir. I miss my wife and I have a
loss for love unfortunately

                              KROUSE

The prisoners are unfortunate

                              SNYDER

Egocentrism?

                              KROUSE

I believe you got caught

                              SNYDER

How long do I need to keep these experiments
going?

                              KROUSE

Keep doing what you're doing until I otherwise
tell you

                              SNYDER

You can invite yourself out sir

                              KROUSE

Thank you, good day Colonel

Krouse exits the office.

INT. HALLWAY - DAY

Krouse steps out of Snyder's office and into the hallway. Hernandez is
standing by the door. Krouse begins to walk down the hall and stops
once Hernandez speaks to him.

                           HERNANDEZ

Hey doc, I got an idea. You should hypnotize
all of these hot bitches into wanting me. They'd
be all over me. I'm ugly holmes

Krouse looks at him dumbfounded.

HERNANDEZ (CONT'D)

Physically, you know what I'm sayin'?

Krouse turns around and continues his walk down the hallway.

INT. BREAK ROOM - DAY

Pendengrob and Shatzi enter the break room.

SHATZI

> I hope you know that I am extremely upset with you Corporal Pendengrob. You were inappropriate and embarrassed me

Pendengrob stares at the vending machine.

PENDENGROB

> Should I get potato chips or a candy bar? Candy bar

Pendengrob deposits change into the vending machine.

SHATZI

> Are you listening to me?

PENDENGROB

No

SHATZI

You are a complete disgrace to our militant force! If Snyder saw you out there today he would be very unhappy with you. I was trying to run things in a respectable manner and you ruined everything that I have worked for

PENDENGROB

What are you talking about?

SHATZI

I am not your mother! I am your superior, but
I'm sure if your mother were here right now she
would be very disappointed in you as well

PENDENGROB

What? You're my superior?

SHATZI

Yes, I am Sergeant Shatzi, second commanding
officer in charge

Pendengrob is sitting at the table and he takes out two guns and
points them at Pendengrob.

PENDENGROB

Are you my superior now?

SHATZI

What are you doing?

PENDENGROB

I'm not doing anything

SHATZI

Put the guns down

PENDENGROB

Which one?

SHATZI

Both of them

PENDENGROB

Why?

SHATZI

Put them down now

PENDENGROB

Do you want to see me pull the trigger?

SHATZI

No I do not

Pendengrob fires a shot at Shatzi, but misses.

SHATZI (CONT'D)

Oh my God, I can't believe you almost shot me!

PENDENGROB

I can't believe I missed.

Snyder enters the break room.

SNYDER

What is going on here?

SHATZI

Corporal Pendengrob tried to kill me!

PENDENGROB

I did not

SHATZI

Yes, he did! He aimed his guns right at me and
fired a shot! He tried to kill me!

PENDENGROB

I was joking around

SHATZI

Colonel Snyder sir! I request that you remove
Corporal Pendengrob from this camp at once.
He is a threat to us all

PENDENGROB

You're the threat

SHATZI

I am not a threat!

SNYDER

Both of you be quiet. I don't know what
happened in here, but I want this mischief to
stop. The general will be here in two weeks and
everything must be concise, no mistakes or else
there will be serious consequences

Snyder begins to exit the break room.

PENDENGROB

When you say serious consequences, how
serious are you?

SNYDER

Very serious

Snyder exits the break room. Shatzi gets in Pendengrob's face.

SHATZI

I am getting sick and tired of your attitude and
lack of respect Pendengrob and I swear that one
day I am going to kill you

Shatzi exits the break room.

INT. BARRACK TWO - NIGHT

Jansdalter enters barrack two and walks over to Freya.

JANSDALTER

We need to talk, come with me

Freya and Jansdalter exit the barrack.

INT. BARRACK EIGHT - NIGHT

Freya and Jansdalter enter the barrack together.

FREYA

What is it?

JANSDALTER

I found out about your husband, he's alive

FREYA

He is?

JANSDALTER

There's a problem

FREYA

What problem?

JANSDALTER

The camp has been torturing him on a daily
basis

FREYA

Torture? So what have they been doing?

JANSDALTER

Colonel Snyder has led some kind of experiment. I don't know what the meaning behind it is, but he has been beaten, burned, whipped and mauled on a daily basis

Freya is speechless.

JANSDALTER (CONT'D)

Do you need to sit down?

FREYA

Yeah

Jansdalter gets a chair and brings it over to Freya, she sits in it.

JANSDALTER

Are you ok?

FREYA

No, I think I'm pretty far from being ok. So, how long has this been going on?

JANSDALTER

A long time, I'm not sure

FREYA

How does he look? I mean...

JANSDALTER

Pretty bad, but he is surviving

FREYA

Cedric, I don't know what to do. I mean you come in here and tell me my husband is being tortured and I'm starving as it is. Would you be willing to help me find a way out of here?

JANSDALTER

There's no way out. The camp keeps a tight check on everybody. All I can say is that I'll keep a close eye on him. I can bring him food and care for him

FREYA

What can I say? Thanks. I don't know what I'd do without you

JANSDALTER

You're welcome, I'll keep you up to date on him

Freya gives Jansdalter a hug.

EXT. NORDFELS ENTRANCE - DAY

A car pulls up to the camp entrance. A line of soldiers are standing in front of the gate. A chauffeur gets out of the car and opens the back passenger door. General Haku gets out of the car. He is an older Asian man wearing a black uniform, hat, monocle, and cape. He carries a cane. Hernandez is standing at the end of the line with Pendengrob.

HERNANDEZ
(To Pendengrob)
I can't believe it; he's wearing a cape man. What is he, a superhero or something?

The general walks past the line of soldiers and the men salute him as he passes by, except for Pendengrob, who stands and does nothing to acknowledge his presence. The general stops in front of Pendengrob.

HAKU

My my my, would you look at this. What a fine example of quality. Your shirt isn't buttoned, your hat is on crooked, you haven't shaved for a good time, oh, and you have a bottle of liquor. Impressive

Snyder comes running to the rescue.

SNYDER

Hello General, very good of you to be here. I have you know that Corporal Pendengrob is one of the finest snipers in our military

HAKU

Pendengrob, I suppose the name does sound familiar. Corporal Larry Pendengrob is it? You claim to be the man who killed 200 men

PENDENGROB

237 in one sitting

HAKU

Oh, 237; pardon me sir I can smell the alcohol on your breath. Is this the way you let your men go around Colonel?

SNYDER

No sir, Pendengrob is a valuable man

HAKU

You should clean up your act soldier; that is what leads to abjection

Snyder and Haku walk through the entrance gates.

                    HAKU (CONT'D)

I have been impressed with you Colonel. I
have seen nothing but good things. This camp
is producing as well as many of the country's
manufacturers

                    SNYDER

I am grateful for business general

                    HAKU

Well you are an excellent leader, don't humble
yourself Colonel

                    SNYDER

Thank you general Haku, we have a great
evening planned for you tonight

                    HAKU

I am looking forward to it. We could all use a
little recreation

INT. SECTION B, BARRACK EIGHT - NIGHT

The barrack is decorated for the party. There is food, punch, and
alcohol. The officers are dressed snazzy in full black uniforms. There
are women dressed in dresses. Pendengrob and a group of men and
women sit at a table. They have all had a little much to drink.

                    PENDENGROB

So I says to the man, I says, she has a peg leg,
she has a damned wooden stick for a leg, and,
and I got a splinter in my foot!

Pendengrob starts laughing uncontrollably and so do all of the soldiers and women sitting with him. Snyder and Haku sit together alone and completely sober.

                    HAKU

    That is a very fine piano you have sitting over there

                    SNYDER

    Yes, that piano was a gift from my wife

                    HAKU

    Are we going to listen to it?

                    SNYDER

    Yes, as a matter of fact I have arranged for a pianist to be here

                    HAKU

    Oh, where is he?

                    SNYDER

    I do not know, excuse me for a moment general

Snyder walks over to Hernandez, who is casually standing and talking to guests.

                SNYDER (CONT'D)

    Hernandez

                HERNANDEZ

    Yes sir

                    SNYDER

    Do you have any word on the pianist?

HERNANDEZ

Yes sir, he sent a message. He can't make it
tonight

SNYDER

What? Why?

HERNANDEZ

His flight has a layover. There is a blizzard. I
got the message five minutes ago

SNYDER

Do you know how to play?

HERNANDEZ

I'm Latin holmes, I don't know about any piano
man. I know that may not mean anything, but
I'm drunk off my asso yo'

SNYDER

Find me someone who does. I don't care who,
anybody

HERNANDEZ

Yes sir

Snyder walks over to Haku and takes a seat next to him. Hernandez
walks up to Jansdalter.

HERNANDEZ (CONT'D)

Cedric, do you know how to play that piano?

JANSDALTER

No, why?

HERNANDEZ

Snyder told me to find someone who can play.
The pianist isn't here yo'

JANSDALTER

I know someone who can play

HERNANDEZ

Really, who?

INT. ROOM THIRTEEN - NIGHT

Jansdalter and Hernandez are holding on to Alurich, who is dressed
in a tuxedo. They put on his cummerbund and straighten his bow-
tie.

HERNANDEZ

Are you sure this is the only person who can
play man?

JANSDALTER

Yes, I'm sure of it, he's incredible

HERNANDEZ

Look at him, he can't even stand. How the hell
is he going to put on a show yo'?

JANSDALTER

He can, I know his wife

HERNANDEZ

Say what? You say you know his what?

JANSDALTER

Trust me

INT. BARRACK EIGHT - NIGHT

The party is still in full swing. Music comes on over the speakers.
Everyone is drunk.

PENDENGROB

Oh, it's my favorite song, would you care to
dance?

OFFICER

I thought you would never ask

Pendengrob and the officer walk out to the dance floor. They dance
around foolishly and everyone laughs at them. Pendengrob grabs the
officer's buttocks as Shatzi enters the barrack.

SHATZI

There will be no homosexual activity here at
Nordfels!

SNYDER

Shatzi

SHATZI

Yes sir!

SNYDER

Sit down

SHATZI

Yes sir!

Shatzi takes a seat in a chair next to Snyder and Haku. Jansdalter and
Hernandez enter the barrack with Alurich. A shocked Snyder walks
over to them.

SNYDER

What in the hell are you thinking?

Pendengrob and the Officer stop dancing when the music ends. Everyone claps for them loudly.

HERNANDEZ

He knows how to play

HAKU

Oh great, is this the pianist?

Jansdalter and Hernandez escort Alurich to the piano. Alurich sits down in front of the piano and stares at it.

HAKU (CONT'D)

Why isn't he playing?

SNYDER

Well as an artist he has to take everything in before he starts

HAKU

He looks shattered, dead, and numbed. What happened to him?

SNYDER

He's extremely tired, rough flight

Alurich taps a few piano keys and then begins playing. He plays the musical piece beautifully and to perfection. Everyone is stunned by his immaculate playing. Haku stands up and claps for him.

HAKU

That was a very fine presentation, I must admit sir. I didn't catch your name?

Alurich does not respond.

                    HAKU (CONT'D)
        Why is he not answering me?

                    SNYDER
        He's a mute

                    ALURICH
        No, I am not a mute. My name is Alurich
        Korall, and I'm a prisoner at this camp

                    HAKU
        Prisoner? Is this true?

                    SNYDER
        No, I mean, how could that be possible? It's not

Alurich continues to stare lifeless at the piano. Jansdalter and
Hernandez help carry Alurich out of the barrack.

                    HAKU
        I think I've had enough partying for tonight, I
        bid you adieu

General Haku exits the barrack.

INT. UNDERGROUND CELL - NIGHT

Jansdalter and Hernandez carry Alurich down to the cell and
chain him to the cement wall. Hernandez exits the cell afterwards.
Jansdalter begins cleaning Alurich's face in the dark.

                    ALURICH
        Who are you?

JANSDALTER

My name is Cedric Jansdalter and I'm here to
help you

ALURICH

How is my face?

JANSDALTER

It isn't that bad

ALURICH

Are you lying?

JANSDALTER

No, I'd tell you. You heal very well

ALURICH

Why do you keep me blindfolded?

JANSDALTER

I don't know, I just follow orders

Hernandez enters with a plate of food and then exits the cell.
Jansdalter places the plate on the floor in front of Alurich.

ALURICH

That smells good. Have you been ordered to
feed me?

JANSDALTER

No, this is my doing

ALURICH

I would be careful if I were you

Jansdalter gives Alurich a plastic fork and he begins eating the turkey and mashed potatoes.

JANSDALTER

I have spoken to your wife. She asked me to keep an eye on you

ALURICH

How do you know my wife?

JANSDALTER

We have grown close, like you and I

ALURICH

I am not close to you

JANSDALTER

I know I am the closest thing to a friend you have, hurry up and eat

Jansdalter takes a can of beer out of his jacket and gives it to Alurich. He drinks the beer and finishes the food.

ALURICH

That was good. Thank you

Jansdalter takes the plate and can with him and begins to exit the cell up the stairs.

ALURICH (CONT'D)

How long will I be here?

JANSDALTER

I don't know

Jansdalter exits the underground cell.

EXT. NORDFELS ENTRANCE - DAY

There is a black car sitting in front of the camp entrance. Snyder walks up to the car and the dark window rolls down. Haku is sitting in the back passenger seat. There is a chauffeur in the driver's seat,

HAKU

Well Colonel, I must admit I was impressed with your work here until I was insulted. The idea that you had one of your own prisoners play before me was demeaning. I'm sure the despot is going to enjoy hearing about my experience at Nordfels when I speak with him. Thank you, good day sir

Haku rolls up the window and the black car drives away.

INT. SNYDER'S OFFICE - DAY

Hernandez and two officers enter Snyder's office. Pendengrob, Jansdalter, and Shatzi are standing by the door. Snyder is sitting at his desk.

HERNANDEZ

You wanted to see us sir?

SNYDER

I'm glad I have all of you here

HERNANDEZ

What's going on?

SNYDER

It seems that the general was unhappy with his visit here due to our irresponsibility

PENDENGROB

What? Me?

SNYDER

All of us, it is just as much my fault for the
controversy. Now we need to make it up to him

PENDENGROB

How?

SNYDER

I plan to take a hundred captives from our
camp and bury them alive. We will march to
the country and have them dig a hole into the
ground large enough to sustain their bodies. We
will film the entire event as a means of social
propaganda.

HERNANDEZ

Nobody wants to watch that man. This is
stupid, crazy

PENDENGROB

Can I be director?

SNYDER

I know of a perfect place thirteen miles from
here. I have ordered two of the newest cameras
on the market and Jansdalter will be in charge of
the film making since he has the experience in
photography.

JANSDALTER

Who do we take?

SNYDER

Barracks one and two from the men and
women; these prisoners are old and their work
can show for it. I will leave the first Lieutenant
in charge while we are gone

PENDENGROB

I've got to admit Snyder, this is complete
madness

SNYDER

No, it's better than that, its art

EXT. COUNTRYSIDE - DAY

Everyone is standing in a large open area surrounded by trees. The
weather is damp and cold. There is a line of female prisoners and
a line of male prisoners. Freya is standing in line with the women.
Freya notices a blindfolded man standing in line off to the distance.

FREYA

Alurich

Freya runs to Alurich and tackles him. They fall to the ground
together. Freya rips the blindfold off and begins kissing him all over
his face.

FREYA (CONT'D)

Alurich! I thought you might have been dead!

An officer comes up behind Freya and hits her in the back of her head
with his rifle. She passes out and falls to the ground. The officer
drags her away. Another officer walks over and attempts to shoot
Alurich with his pistol before Snyder swipes his arm away. The officer
fires a shot, but misses Alurich. Snyder slaps the officer in the face.

SNYDER

You will not shoot him or any other person
involved

Snyder lifts Alurich up off the ground and places the blindfold over
his eyes.

SNYDER (CONT'D)

This man is to remain blindfolded at all times

Hernandez walks up to Snyder.

HERNANDEZ

Colonel, there's someone here to see you sir

INT. SNYDER'S TENT - DAY

There is a woman standing inside of Snyder's tent with a camera man
and sound operator. Snyder takes a seat at his table.

SNYDER

May I help you?

LYNDA

Hello Colonel, I'm news reporter Lynda
Leiberman and I'm here doing a story on the
activities at your camp. I arrived there earlier
today and was told that you were here

SNYDER

I'm sorry, but there must be a mistake. The
government has made it clear that no media is
allowed inside any of the camp sites.

LYNDA

If you don't mind me saying so I think this

entire thing stinks of illegal activity. These prisoners are obviously mistreated. Is the convention aware of this?

SNYDER

I assure you that nothing being done here is illegal. The nation is well aware of everything that is happening concerning the war and our captives.

LYNDA

These captives are our own people. I don't understand. I have been broadcasting for over ten years and I have never seen anything like this. It looks like you're engaged in genocide of our nation's own citizens as well as the enemies we have taken. What is going on here? Where is your authority?

SNYDER

I am the authority. The citizens of our nation are the worlds finest

LYNDA

I have you know Colonel that I have the right to report on anything that may interest the public. The constitution states that anything...

SNYDER

You can report on anything that you wish, but it will never be released to the public

LYNDA

And if I do?

SNYDER

I will personally have your bodies burned along
with your footage, and nobody will ever know
what happened to you

LYNDA

I am going to get to the bottom of this Colonel

SNYDER

You will be dead

Lynda Leiberman and her crew exit the tent.

EXT. COUNTRYSIDE - DAY

There are prisoners tied together with chains digging. Lynda
Leiberman and her crew get into their van and drive off.

HERNANDEZ

What was that all about?

SNYDER

I let her go

INT. WOMEN'S TENT - NIGHT

Freya, Elise, and Beth are inside the tent with several other women.
Freya regains consciousness and Beth helps her up.

FREYA

What happened?

BETH

You were hit in the head dear

FREYA

I saw Alurich and then I ran to him

ELISE

Then you were hit over the head with a rifle and now you're in here while we've been out digging all day

FREYA

Digging?

BETH

They brought us all the way out here in this freezing cold to dig for them

FREYA

What are we digging?

BETH

We don't know. We're going to make an escape tonight, are you coming?

FREYA

What about the guards?

ELISE

We'll take our chances. It's the only way out Freya. If we stay they'll kill us any ways

FREYA

I can't leave Alurich

ELISE

Are you sure about that?

FREYA

Maybe there's a way we can get him

ELISE

Oh God Freya, men come and go, we need to
get out of here

FREYA

I love him

BETH

I understand you love Alurich very much Freya,
like I loved your father, but if we're going to try
an escape we need to do it now or never because
we might not be alive tomorrow

FREYA

I'm staying

There is a long pause, and then Beth and Freya hug.

INT. OFFICER'S TENT - NIGHT

Shatzi, Hernandez, Jansdalter, and Pendengrob are lying in the dark
on the floor asleep. Pendengrob is snoring loudly and wakes Shatzi,
who turns on the light.

SHATZI

Would you shut up!

JANSDALTER

I didn't say anything

SHATZI

Not you, him!

Shatzi shakes Pendengrob and wakes him.

SHATZI (CONT'D)
(In Pendengrob's face)
Shut up!!!!

PENDENGROB
What? What?

SHATZI
You have been snoring all night!

PENDENGROB
What?

SHATZI
I want you to stop!

PENDENGROB
I will...

Pendengrob falls back asleep and Shatzi turns the light off. Moments later Pendengrob starts snoring again. Shatzi turns the light back on and heads outside with his sleeping bag.

SHATZI
Impossible!

HERNANDEZ
Where are you going?

SHATZI
I'm going outside!

HERNANDEZ

Turn the light off

SHATZI

I swear Pendengrob that one day I am going to
kill you

HERNANDEZ

He can't hear you, he's out

Shatzi exits the tent.

EXT. WOMEN'S TENT - NIGHT

Beth and Elise are sneaking out of the back of their tent. The guard
watching the tent doesn't notice them. The women start running
towards the abandoned forest and Elise stops. She motions to Shatzi,
who is in front of the officer's tent with his sleeping bag and assault
rifle.

ELISE

(Shouting) Shatzi!!!

Shatzi hears Elise and drops his sleeping bag. He shoots Beth and
Joanne, who fall to the ground and die.

INT. WOMEN'S TENT - NIGHT

All of the women in the tent are awakened. Freya is both shocked
and frightened.

EXT. COUNTRYSIDE - NIGHT

All of the officers are standing in the middle of all the tents. Two officers drag Beth and Joanne over to Snyder, who is standing beside Shatzi and Elise. Snyder speaks into a megaphone.

> SNYDER
>
> In case any of you were wondering that noise was the sound of two of our female patrons trying to escape. They were killed on sight

INT. WOMEN'S TENT - NIGHT

Freya is listening to Snyder.

EXT. COUNTRYSIDE - NIGHT

> SNYDER
>
> We will leave them in the middle of the field as a reminder to you all. Tomorrow will be a long day so it is important that we all get our rest tonight

INT. WOMEN'S TENT - NIGHT

Freya lies down on the ground and attempts to fall asleep.

EXT. COUNTRYSIDE – DAY

The scene opens with a bird's eye view wide angle shot of the giant hole and all of the prisoners digging. There are four bulldozers plowing into the ground helping them. Snyder is on a hill driving golf balls. Jansdalter and a male prisoner are standing beside him. Snyder drives a ball far away.

> SNYDER
>
> That was a good shot

The prisoner runs away and fetches the ball as Snyder lays another one down on a tee. An officer walks up to Snyder.

> OFFICER

The hole has been completed as you requested sir. They are ready

> SNYDER

Place them around the hole and tie their hands together. Park the dozers behind them. I'll be there shortly

> OFFICER

Yes sir

The officer walks away and Snyder takes his black lacquer watch out of his pocket, checks the time, kisses the watch and then places it back into his pocket.

> JANSDALTER

I always see you carrying the watch around. You always kiss it, why?

> SNYDER

That watch is a gift from someone who loves me very much

> JANSDALTER

It's very nice. Who gave it to you?

The prisoner returns with Snyder's golf ball and Snyder drives another ball far away. The prisoner fetches it.

> SNYDER

My wife

JANSDALTER

Do you love her?

SNYDER

Love cannot exist now, maybe at a later time.
You know Cedric, out of all the help I have, I
must say that you are my favorite. You're not
a pain in the ass and that's why I like you Mr.
Jansdalter

JANSDALTER

Thank you sir

SNYDER

Go help the others get the prisoners ready.
Prepare the film

JANSDALTER

Yes sir

Jansdalter walks away and Snyder drives another ball off to the side.
Jansdalter walks over to Freya, who is digging with the rest of the
prisoners. She notices Beth and Joanne off in a distance lying on
the ground in a bare field surrounded by tents. She then notices
Alurich, who is blindfolded and digging in a distance. The officers
are beginning to line the prisoners up around the hole.

FREYA

Cedric Jansdalter sir, I'm so sorry that you have
to be a part of this; I need to be tied to my
husband. Will you do that for me?

Jansdalter removes Freya from her chains and escorts her to the
beginning of the line and ties her to an old man's wrist with rope. He
walks over to Alurich and escorts him to Freya. He ties Alurich to
Freya. Their wrists are connected at the end of the line with a piece
of twine rope.

FREYA (CONT'D)

Thank you Jansdalter

Jansdalter quietly walks away.

FREYA (CONT'D)

Alurich, we're tied in a line and your at the end
of it

Alurich doesn't say anything.

FREYA (CONT'D)

They killed mother last night

ALURICH

I know, I heard everything, I'm sorry, I loved her
and she will be missed. What are they doing
with us?

FREYA

I don't know, but I asked to be tied to you

ALURICH

I love you

FREYA

I love you too

Elise is dressed in a soldier's black uniform. She is tying the hands of
prisoners a few feet away from Freya.

FREYA (CONT'D)

I see you! I see you Elise! You think you're
bad? Huh? I know you can hear me evil bitch!
(Screaming) How could you!

Elise coldly stares at Freya and then walks away.

FREYA (CONT'D)

I don't understand

ALURICH

Don't question her. Rationality is dead

Snyder is standing in the back of the prisoners with Jansdalter by his side.

SNYDER

It looks like we're about set. Where is Hernandez?

JANSDALTER

He's over by the forestry, the trees

SNYDER

What? Go get him

JANSDALTER

Yes sir

EXT. FOREST - DAY

Hernandez is carving his initials into a tree with a knife. Jansdalter walks up to him.

JANSDALTER

Come on, it's time to start. Snyder is waiting

Hernandez finishes his carving and stabs his knife into the tree and leaves it there. They both walk away.

EXT. COUNTRYSIDE - DAY

Jansdalter and Hernandez walk over to Snyder. All of the soldiers are standing around the line of prisoners. Jansdalter takes the handheld camera out of the bag and places it on his shoulder. Snyder speaks into the megaphone.

SNYDER

March them

The prisoners start walking towards the giant hole and the bulldozers follow behind them. All of the prisoners are tied together at the wrists and form a line. Once they reach the hole everyone stops. The prisoners surround the hole and there is a long moment of silence.

SNYDER (CONT'D)

Bury them, bury them all

The bulldozers push the prisoners into the giant hole. The prisoners to the right fall in first followed by those to the left. The gravitational force causes all of the prisoners to fall in at once. Snyder takes a conductor's stick and begins waving it around like a conductor of an orchestra. The bulldozers plow dirt through the prisoners and into the giant man made crater. Many of the prisoners attempt to hold the side of ground for support. The officers smash the prisoner's hands with shovels to allow for their entombment. Jansdalter films the entire event with his hand-held camera. The scene switches consistently between Jandalter's hand-held version to the original tripod and dolly version. Alurich and Freya are the final prisoners to fall into the hole as the line's heaviness of people forces them in. Alurich holds on to the edge of the earth with his left hand and clinches the weight of prisoners with his right. Freya and the old man become disconnected as the rope that held them together at the wrist snaps. The old man falls into the cluttered hole and is engulfed by dirt. The bulldozers continue to fill the hole with dirt and bury the prisoners. Alurich continues to hold onto the side of the earth with his left hand and Freya with his right. The old man rises from the dirt and grabs Freya's legs as he holds on to her. Alurich doesn't have the strength to hold the weight of both. Alurich and Freya's rope snaps. They are no longer tied at the wrist.

FREYA
(Screaming)

Alurich!

ALURICH
(Screaming)

I'm trying!

FREYA
(Screaming at the old man)
Get off me!

The old man continues to hold Freya's legs for his life. An officer smashes Alurich's hand with a shovel. His hand breaks, but he still holds onto the earth. Alurich loses grip of Freya and the several others tied to the old man. All of the prisoners except for Alurich sink into the dirt. Freya is drowned by the dirt and engulfed into the black hole.

ALURICH
(Shouting)

Freya!

Alurich molds his hands into the side of the earth while the bulldozers continue to fill the giant man made pit. Eventually, the hole is completely filled. An overhead shot shows Snyder standing alone atop the dirt filled crater. He walks away and exits the scene.

EXT. NORDFELS CAMP - DAY

WIDE ANGLE: BIRD'S EYE ESTABLISHING
SHOT OF NORDFELS

INT. BREAK ROOM - DAY

Snyder, Jansdalter, Pendengrob, and Elise enter the break room dressed in full black uniforms.

> SNYDER
>
> Ms. Elise, I have a ticket for your departure. I will have much to say about your work here, thank you. I'm sure that your husband will be excited to see you. When you arrive tell the ambassador I give my appreciation

They shake hands.

> ELISE
>
> My pleasure Colonel

> SNYDER
>
> Well accomplished my spy

Snyder walks away and the drunken Pendengrob walks up to the beautiful Elise.

> PENDENGROB
>
> Ahhh, my beautiful woman; I love a woman in uniform. Let's go do it. Let me frisk you

> ELISE
>
> Larry, if you were the last man on the planet I wouldn't. If there was a bomb shelter and we were stuck inside and we couldn't get out because of the radiation, I wouldn't. I would rather fry, oh, you smell

> PENDENGROB
> (Frisking her)

What? Come on, good, I'm not the last man;
we're not in a bomb shelter. Give it to me

ELISE
(Pushing him off)
Get away

Elise walks away from Pendengrob. Jansdalter walks up to
Pendengrob.

PENDENGROB

She's got my heart

Jansdalter begins to exit the break room.

SNYDER

Corporal Jansdalter sir, I need pictures of the
new inventory in the gas chamber. Get on it
immediately

JANSDALTER

Yes sir

Jansdalter exits the break room.

INT. CAMP RESTROOM

Jansdalter enters the camp restroom. He enters a stall and closes the
door. A gunshot is heard. Blood begins creeping slowly on the floor
and out of the closed stall. Moments later, Snyder, Pendengrob, and
Shatzi enter the restroom. Snyder attempts to open the locked stall
door, but in unsuccessful. He kicks the stall door open and Jansdalter
is sitting on the toilet dead with a gun in his hand and a hole in the
back of his head.

SNYDER

Where's the film? Where's the film!?

Snyder pushes Jansdalter onto the floor as he searches for the film. Pendengrob, Shatzi, and Snyder stare at the toilet bowl. Snyder charges out of the restroom.

PENDENGROB

I hope he didn't clog the toilet

EXT. COUNTRYSIDE - DAY

The camera looms above the ground where the prisoners were buried moments ago. Freezing raindrops and sleet slam the damp snow covered ground. A hand looms from the freshly covered ground as lightning strikes the background with a thunderous roar.

INT. CAMP RESTROOM - DAY

Snyder, Pendengrob, and Shatzi stand in front of the stall. Jansdalter lies on the ground dead swimming in his own pool of blood. Snyder attempts to recover the film from the toilet with a plunger, but is continually unsuccessful. He angrily marches out of the restroom with nervous authority.

SNYDER

Shatzi, gather me thirteen prisoners and bring
them to the break room immediately

SHATZI

Yes sir!

EXT. CAMP ENTRY - DAY

The rain and ice continue to fall outside the camp gates. Alurich walks up to the camp gates dazed in soaking mud. He stares at the two officers standing in the watchtower with his hands in the air.

OFFICER #1

Who is that?

The second officer shoots Alurich in the chest with his assault rifle. Alurich falls to the ground. The officers open the camp gates and march down the watchtower ladder. Both of them walk up to Alurich.

OFFICER #1 (CONT'D)

Is he dead?

OFFICER #2

Yeah, he's dead

OFFICER #1

He's not bleeding

OFFICER #2

I got him right through the heart, help me

Both of the officers close the camp gates, lift Alurich from the ground, and carry him to barrack 13, Section A.

EXT. SECTION A, BARRACK THIRTEEN - DAY

There is an officer standing in front of barrack thirteen smoking a cigarette and drinking a bottle of water. The two officers on duty from the watchtower carry Alurich into the barrack and moments later they exit.

OFFICER #3

Hey! What the hell is this?

OFFICER #2

He's dead

OFFICER #3

Well don't just leave him in there!

OFFICER #1

No, you do it, can't

Both of the watchtower officers walk away.

OFFICER #3

Where you guys going? I'm telling Snyder!

Both of the officers continue to walk away. The officer on watch duty throws his cigarette to the ground and enters barrack thirteen.

INT. SECTION A, BARRACK THIRTEEN - DAY

The officer enters the barrack. Alurich is lying on the table motionless. The officer walks over to Alurich and places his head on Alurich's chest as he checks for a heartbeat. Alurich takes out Hernandez's knife from his pocket and stabs the officer in the back of the neck. The officer and Alurich fall to the ground together. Alurich covers the officer's mouth and the men struggle. The officer eventually dies. Alurich stands and looks around the room.

INT. SECTION A, BARRACK FIFTEEN - DAY

Pendengrob and Shatzi search the barrack and randomly check the productivity of parts. Pendengrob turns and Shatzi stabs him in the stomach with his knife. Pendengrob holds onto Shatzi for support.

SHATZI

I always told you that one day I was going to kill you and today is that day. I have always hated you in disgust for your lack of respect. I give everyone a gift with your death. Are you becoming weak?

Pendengrob falls to the ground and dies. Shatzi exits the barrack.

INT. BREAK ROOM - DAY

Shatzi enters the break room with thirteen male prisoners. He lines the prisoners against the wall.

SNYDER

Pendengrob? Where is Corporal Pendengrob?

SHATZI

I can get him at your request sir

SNYDER

Yes, please, get him

SHATZI

Sir!

Shatzi exits the break room.

INT. SECTION A, BARRACK FIFTEEN - DAY

Shatzi enters the barrack and Pendengrob is lying on the floor, dead in a pool of blood.

SHATZI
(Shouting)
Corporal Pendengrob! Colonel Snyder demands
that you come to the break room at once!

Pendengrob continues to lie dead on the floor.

SHATZI(CONT'D)

Did you hear me Corporal Pendengrob? I said

that Colonel Hugo Snyder demands that you
come to the break room at once!

Pendengrob continues to lie dead on the floor.

SHATZI (CONT'D)
(Shouting)
Fine! Just lie on the floor and ignore me! See
if I care! Completely disrespectful! Colonel
Snyder is going to be very upset with you!

Shatzi marches perfectly out of the barrack.

INT. BREAK ROOM - DAY

Shatzi marches into the break room. The thirteen male prisoners are
still standing motionless against the wall. Snyder stands in front of
them.

SNYDER

Where is he?

SHATZI

He is in barrack fifteen, section A. I attempted
to bring him here at your request sir, but he
insisted to lie on the floor and ignore me

SNYDER

He must be intoxicated. I feel that I will be
forced to take disciplinary action this time

SHATZI

Sir!

Snyder takes out his handgun and attempts to fire shots at the
prisoners, but his gun is jammed. The prisoners continue to stand
against the wall motionless without any facial reaction.

SNYDER

Damn, my gun is jammed

Shatzi quickly marches over to Snyder and offers him his assault rifle.

SHATZI

It would be an honor if you would be so kind to
use my gun sir!

Snyder takes Shatzi's assault rifle and aims it at the motionless
prisoners, but doesn't fire.

SNYDER

I do not want to kill these men. Take them
back

SHATZI

What are you talking about sir? Kill them!

SNYDER

No, get them out of here

Shatzi dramatically marches back to the prisoners in disbelief.

SHATZI

Come on! You heard the Colonel! Move it!
Get the hell out of here!

Shatzi and the prisoners exit the break room.

INT. HALLWAY - DAY

Alurich is slowly walking down the hall dressed in full black uniform
with a half emptied bottle of water in his hand. He passes by Shatzi,
who continually harasses and yells at the thirteen prisoners walking
by.

INT. BREAK ROOM - DAY

Snyder is standing by the vending machine and places change inside of it. The vending machine doesn't dispense his purchase. Snyder fires several rounds into the vending machine glass with Shatzi's assault rifle. The glass shatters and Snyder cautiously takes out a bag of chips. He sits down at a nearby table.

INT. HALLWAY - DAY

Alurich approaches the break room.

INT. BREAK ROOM - DAY

Snyder is sitting alone in the break room eating a sandwich and a bag of chips.

INT. HALLWAY - DAY

Alurich finishes drinking the bottle of water and places it over the barrel of the officer's gun that he just killed. He wraps tape around the gun and quietly enters the break room.

INT. BREAK ROOM - DAY

Alurich walks over to Snyder and places the gun to the side of his head. Snyder notices Alurich, dressed in full black uniform, face covered in dirt, looking like the walking dead, and is dumbfounded. Snyder stares at Alurich in a trance, who speaks in a cold and dead voice.

ALURICH

You thought it would be over. You are wrong

Alurich fires a shot through Snyder's head. The plastic bottle silences the shot. Snyder falls out of his chair, hits the ground, and dies instantly.

CUT TO:

INT. GAS CHAMBER - DAY

Hernandez, Shatzi, and four other officers are doing a body count inside the chamber. Dead bodies lie all over the chamber floor. The steel chamber door is wide open, and can be seen in the background. Suddenly, the chamber door slams shut and all of the men stop in their tracks. Shatzi walks over to the closed chamber door and stares out the window. Alurich's face appears out of nowhere. Shatzi is stunned. Poisonous gas begins to mist out of the chamber piping. Shatzi begins to panic.

SHATZI
(Shouting)
Open! Open this door now!

Shatzi takes an assault rifle out of the grip of a fellow officer's grasp and fires several shots at the glass, but the bulletproof glass doesn't shatter. Shatzi throws the assault rifle down to the ground and begins to frantically pound on the steel door. Alurich continues to stare at him indifferently.

SHATZI (CONT'D)
(Crying)
Let me out!

Alurich continues to stare in lifeless manner at Shatzi. The camera moves from Alurich's side of the wall where there is complete silence across to the gas chamber, where all of the men are yelling and begging for their lives among the dead. The officers fall to the ground and die slowly one by one.

CUT TO:

INT. CHAMBER ENTRANCE - DAY

Alurich is leaning against the wall unconscious.

INT. GAS CHAMBER - DAY

The chamber door opens and the soldiers dressed in white uniforms, headed by their lieutenant, enter the chamber.

> LIEUTENANT
> (Sniffing)
> You never quite get used to the smell. Ok, tag em' and bag em' boys!

The soldiers dressed in white uniforms begin to gather all of the dead bodies.

> WHITE SOLDIER
> Sir, you need to come check this out

INT. CHAMBER ENTRANCE - DAY

Alurich is lying on the ground in full black uniform leaning against the wall unconscious. Two soldiers dressed in full white uniforms are sitting on the floor next to him.

> LIEUTENANT
> Who is he?

> WHITE SOLDIER
> We don't know. We found him in here when we arrived

> LIEUTENANT
> Any identification?

WHITE SOLDIER

None

LIEUTENANT

Did you get a print?

WHITE SOLDIER #2

(Holding Alurich's hand)

He doesn't have any tips

LIEUTENANT

What do you mean?

WHITE SOLDIER #2

(Showing the Lieutenant Alurich's hand)

I mean he doesn't have any tips

LIEUTENANT

(Taking Alurich's hand)

It looks like he's tried to claw his way out of something

WHITE SOLDIER

You should see his back

LIEUTENANT

Why is he dressed in a black uniform? He's obviously not an officer covered in dirt. Perhaps he can explain all of this

WHITE SOLDIER

This man can't tell us anything about what happened here, he's barely alive

WHITE SOLDIER #2

He's freezing, ice cold

WHITE SOLDIER

You see here that he's been shot. The bullet
must be stuck in him, he hasn't lost any blood.
He's breathing and has a pulse, a slow one, but
his heart is still beating

LIEUTENANT

Ok, this place is a mess, get him out of here.
Take him on the next chopper. Have the medics
take a look at him.
                    (Yelling)
Ricky! Get that chopper ready! We gotta get
movin' on this next one! Everybody listen!
Make sure you have a tag for every body found
before you put them in a bag! There still could
be some alive!

The White Coats carry Alurich out of the chamber entrance room.

EXT. SECTION C - DAY

The White Coats have the Black Coats in custody. They march them
in handcuffs. Elise and several other soldiers dressed in black are
being escorted onto helicopters. There are several helicopters on site.
The two soldiers dressed in white carry Alurich to a helicopter. The
men reach the helicopter and place Alurich inside of it along with
several other famished prisoners.

INT. HELICOPTER - DAY

Alurich leans against the helicopter's wall in a moveable chair.
Alurich takes out Snyder's black lacquer watch from his cloth pocket
and stares at the Tao located on the face.

FADE TO BLACK.

THE BLACK

BOX

PARADOX

TITLE CARD:

'THE BLACK BOX PARADOX'

FADE IN:

EXT. CITY STREETS - DAY

'THE BLACK BOX PARADOX' is shot in color. We PAN across
a gray sky to an old apartment building. The camera descends
down to the streets of an old wrought iron staircase in front of the
building. The camera descends down the stairs to a black steel door.
The camera moves through the door and descends even further down
another old wrought iron staircase and into a concrete cell.

INT. ALURICH'S CELL - DAY

The cell is dark with the only light coming from a small vent at the
top of the ceiling. The camera continues to hover above the concrete
ground and comes up to Alurich, who is lying on a bed with a black
sheet covering his legs. Glowing scorpions crawl over his bare chest
and steel pins cover his face. Alurich opens his eyes, gets out of bed,
and pulls a piece of black string that turns on a dim yellow light
bulb connected to the ceiling. A black grand piano sits against
the wall. A wall of knives and a hanging whip sit along another
wall. An old black ironed stove sits on another wall next to a small
black refrigerator. Alurich walks into the bathroom and turns on the
glowing yellow light.

INT. ALURICH'S BATHROOM - DAY

The small bathroom has a black sink with a mirror above it along
with a black bathtub and black toilet. Alurich looks in the mirror,
takes the pins out of his face, and places the scorpions in a glass case.
He turns the black sink knob and scolding hot water begins pouring
out of the faucet. Alurich places his hands in the sink and splashes

the steaming hot water onto his jagged face without any reaction. He uses a black sponge to paint his jagged face with white clown makeup.

INT. ALURICH'S CELL - SUNSET

Alurich exits the bathroom and walks over to a black clothes rack. All of the clothes on the rack are black. He is wearing black pants and puts on a black shirt. He puts on black socks and black boots. His forearms are covered with scars. He rolls the black sleeves down. He throws on a black leather coat and exits the cell up the stairs.

INT. BAR - SUNSET

Alurich enters the dimly lit bar. There are a few people at the bar casually sitting at tables and enjoying their time. Alurich takes a seat on a black stool in front of the bar. A young man and two attractive young women are sitting behind him.

MICHELLE
(Toward's Alurich)
Circus must be in town

The bartender approaches Alurich.

BARTENDER
What can I get for ya?

ALURICH
Lager

BARTENDER
Any particular kind?

ALURICH
Black

BARTENDER

To match the outfit right?

Alurich ignores him and the bartender brings a glass of black lager.
He sits it on the bar.

STAN

Hey, listen all I said I wanted to do is go to a
place after the movie where we could just chill
and relax and you said this place and now you're
totally hasslin' me

MICHELLE

What!? Well *excuse* me! If you wouldn't have
gotten lost then none of this would have
happened

STAN

Maybe if you knew where we were going then
we wouldn't be stuck in this dump

MICHELLE

This place isn't bad, what's wrong with this
place?

STAN

This place is a doo doo hole. Nobody wants to
be at this place

MICHELLE

What are you scared now Stan? Are you scared
of this place?

STAN

Please, I try to take you girls out and this is the
thanks I get

AMANDA

You guys sound like you're married. I have a
headache

MICHELLE

(Reaching in her purse)
I have pain killers

STAN

I'm going to the bar

Stand takes a seat next to Alurich at the bar.

STAN (CONT'D)

Hey, what's up? What's with the outfit?

Alurich doesn't say anything.

STAN (CONT'D)

Ok, fine, don't wanna talk don't talk. I've been
listening to these two all night. These bitches
man, take em' out, buy em' a few drinks, they
turn into...damned annoying man, but I'm sure
you know what that's all about right?

Alurich doesn't say anything.

STAN (CONT'D)

Yeah, what's with these bitches anyways?
Why can't they just...I don't know...shutup or
something, you know?

Alurich doesn't say anything and continues to drink his black lager. A
crazy looking heavy set middle-aged man enters the bar with a large
handgun dressed in a green trench coat carrying a brown paper bag.

ROBBER

(Shouting)

Ok everybody listen up! I'm robbing this place!
This is what I want! Everybody give me their
wallets! Nobody move! You! Bartender! Open
the register now!

Everyone in the bar lifts their hands up in the air except for Alurich,
who continues to sit motionless and drink his black lager. The robber
walks throughout the bar and takes everyone's wallet.

ROBBER (CONT'D)

(Shouting)

Ok, this is good. Anybody moves I swear I'll
kill them! You better hurry up bartender! I
don't have all day here!

The bartender opens the register and empties the money into the
robber's bag. The robber approaches Stan, who gives him his wallet.
Next, he approaches Alurich.

ROBBER (CONT'D)

You! Give me your wallet!

Alurich doesn't acknowledge the Robber's presence.

ROBBER (CONT'D)

Now!

ALURICH

I do not have a wallet

ROBBER

Then put your money in the bag!

ALURICH

I do not have any money

ROBBER

You've got about two seconds before I blow your head off!

ALURICH

Am I the one you really want to kill? Do you want to kill me? Or do you want to kill yourself? If you kill me then you will be locked up forever. Do us all a favor and put the gun to your own head

The Robber hits Alurich in the head with the revolver of the gun as hard as he can. Alurich doesn't flinch. Black blood begins to flow downwards from Alurich's forehead and onto his face. Alurich swipes the leaking blood with his hand and puts it in his mouth.

ALURICH (CONT'D)

I like the taste of anything that is black

ROBBER
What the hell?

The stunned robber quickly takes off running out of the bar with the bag of money.

MICHELLE
(To Alurich)

Are you ok?

Alurich stands up and walks out of the bar.

EXT. SIDEWALK, CITY STREETS - SUNSET

Alurich walks out of the bar and begins his journey down the sidewalk completely ignoring anyone that is in his path. The camera dollies backwards as he walks forwards and passes several people.

Every person he walks through is angered by his unwillingness to move. First, Alurich bumps into a man dressed in a gray suit.

MAN

Hey, watch it!

Next, Alurich bumps into a provocatively dressed upper class woman who is carrying shopping bags.

WOMAN

Hey! Watch where you're going!

Next, a classic 1950's red car pulls out in front of Alurich. He doesn't move, and steps on the hood of the car and continues to walks in a straight line. A middle-aged man furiously gets out of the car.

MAN #2
(Shouting)
Hey! Watch where you're going! I just had this detailed!

Alurich continues to walk in a straight line and exits the picture on the right side.

EXT. STONE ROCK HOUSE - SUNSET

A small stone rock house sits next to a lake in a rural area surrounded by trees. The sun is setting over the lake. Alurich is the only person around for miles. He drifts leisurely down the stone walkway leading to the house door. He enters the stone rock house with dark blood still on his painted white face.

INT. RED ROOM - SUNSET

Alurich enters a small dimly lit red room with a painted white face and darkened dried blood. All of the walls are painted red. The ceiling and the floor are red as well. There aren't any windows in the room. The dimly glowing yellow light comes from two bulbs located in the corner of the walls. Alurich takes a seat in a white iron chair that sits in the middle of the room. There are two black speakers connected to the walls in front of him. A soft woman's voice comes through the speakers.

WOMAN'S VOICE

Hello, what brings you to me?

Alurich doesn't say anything.

INT. BLACK ROOM - SUNSET

CLOSE-UP: KERRY'S MOUTH

Kerry is a seven year old boy who sits in the black room alone. Only his lips are revealed. He speaks through a microphone with a boy's voice.

KERRY

Is there anything you would like to talk...

INT. RED ROOM - SUNSET

Kerry's sentence is completed through the speakers with the soft woman's voice.

WOMAN'S VOICE

About? Do you have any interests?

ALURICH

...Pain

Alurich rolls his sleeves up.

INT. BLACK ROOM - NIGHT

CLOSE UP: KERRY'S MOUTH

> KERRY
>
> I see

INT. RED ROOM - NIGHT

> ALURICH
>
> I would not call it an interest, an addiction. I am addicted to black. Everything must be black. I am having difficulty sitting in this chair, and the walls...

> WOMAN'S VOICE
>
> And why do you do this to yourself?

> ALURICH
>
> I was a prisoner in the war, conditioned this way. I want to be normal again

INT. BLACK ROOM - NIGHT

CLOSE-UP: KERRY'S MOUTH

> KERRY
>
> Are any of us really...

INT. RED ROOM - NIGHT

> WOMAN'S VOICE
>
> Normal?

> ALURICH

I am not sure. There is a woman. There is
something special about her. She had been in
my dreams consistently for a year. I had never
met her. This woman was at the restaurant
where I eat twice a week. They have black tables
and chairs there, very dim, I can handle it

INT. BLACK ROOM - NIGHT

CLOSE UP: KERRY'S MOUTH

> KERRY

So this woman, are you sure she is the same
woman you dreamed about?

> ALURICH

She is the same

> KERRY

What was she doing there?

> ALURICH

She works there

INT. RED ROOM - NIGHT

> KERRY

How do you feel about this woman?

> ALURICH

I have never spoken to her, but I will. Right
now I am still emotionally battling the past

INT. BLACK ROOM - NIGHT

CLOSE-UP: KERRY'S MOUTH

> KERRY
>
> You are fighting with yourself. Remember, memories don't lie

INT. RED ROOM - NIGHT

> ALURICH
>
> Perhaps she can help me, like you

INT. BLACK ROOM - NIGHT

CLOSE UP: KERRY'S MOUTH

> KERRY
>
> She will, I need you to...

INT. RED ROOM - NIGHT

> WOMAN'S VOICE
>
> Go home and get a good night's sleep

> ALURICH
>
> I will; thank you

Alurich exits the red room.

INT. BAR - NIGHT

One detective and one police officer are interrogating the bar where the robber was at earlier.

                    DETECTIVE

So you say he was wearing all black

                    MICHELLE

Yes, he was dressed in black

                    DETECTIVE

Can you give any other description?

                    STAN

He was about my height, average build. This guy came in here and robbed the place

                    POLICE OFFICER

And what happened?

                    STAN

He just came up to him and hit him in the head with his gun. The guy jetted off with our money

                    POLICE OFFICER

Which guy?

                    STAN

The big guy, the guy with the green trench coat

                    DETECTIVE

Can you describe anything else about the robber, anything unusual about the guy? Any scars, tattoos?

STAN

No, he was just big and tall, you know, like I
said, fat, hairy, dark hair

MICHELLE

He smelled

AMANDA

Yeah, he smelled really bad

DETECTIVE

Any particular kind of odor?

MICHELLE

He smelled like someone who hadn't showered
in a long time

AMANDA

I thought he was going to kill all of us, but he
got scared, in a way that guy in black saved us

DETECTIVE

Ok, we'll keep an eye out for that guy in black
and the robber

POLICE OFFICER

You guys have had a long night

MICHELLE

Tell me about it, I'm like really traumatized

STAN

Would you shut-up

MICHELLE

Stan, we were just robbed

POLICE OFFICER

If you want there's a trauma center we can take
you to

STAN

Yeah, go there and you'll be really messed up

MICHELLE

No, I'm ok; I just want to go home

AMANDA

Yeah, take us home Stan

DETECTIVE

We have everything we need

MICHELLE

Thank you

AMANDA

Thank you officer

Stan, Michelle, and Amanda exit the bar.

POLICE OFFICER

Drive safely

DETECTIVE

This is going to be a long night

The Police Officer speaks into his walkie-talkie.

POLICE OFFICER

We have an eye witness we're looking for, man
dressed in black, white male, six feet, average

build, he might be around this area. Keep a
lookout, over

EXT. ALLEY - NIGHT

A prostitute stands out alone in an inner city alley. Alurich
approaches her.

> ### ALURICH
>
> Where is Crystal?

> ### TRIXIE
>
> I'm Trixie, Crystal's gone baby, and she's never
> coming back. Why? What's wrong with me?
> Am I not good enough for you or something?

> ### ALURICH
>
> Crystal and I had a special kind of relationship

> ### TRIXIE
>
> Well what about having a relationship with
> me baby? I promise I will make your deepest
> fantasies come true

> ### ALURICH
>
> I do not think that you know who you are
> dealing with

> ### TRIXIE
>
> Try me

INT. ALURICH'S CELL - NIGHT

Alurich and Trixie walk down the steps and enter the cell.

TRIXIE

Oh my God, this is where you live? It's freezing in here. Don't you have any heat?

ALURICH

No heat, no pain

TRIXIE

I was counting your steps. Do you know it's exactly 13 steps down here? I am an independent provider you know. The rate we discuss is the rate you pay, no surprises. So what do you want?

ALURICH

You sound like a used car salesman

Alurich hands her his whip from the wall, turns his back, leans against the wall, and takes his shirt off. She sees the burns and scars covering his back.

ALURICH (CONT'D)

Hit me with everything you have

TRIXIE

Uhh, I've never whipped anyone before

ALURICH

There are many men who have never had sexual encounters before. You take their virginity

TRIXIE

What the hell is that supposed to mean?

ALURICH

Do not worry about hurting me

Trixie weakly whips his back once. Alurich is displeased with her lack of motivation. Trixie quickly throws the whip down, runs up the stairs and exits the cell.

INT. RESTAURANT - NIGHT

Alurich enters the restaurant. Mirrors surround the walls with black tables, black chairs, and black carpeting. The employees are dressed in white. The Hostess approaches Alurich, who is dressed in complete black and white clown makeup.

HOSTESS

Hi, how are you? Would you like the usual?

ALURICH
(Pointing to Viktoria)
I would like to sit in her section

HOSTESS

Ok, follow me

Alurich follows the Hostess into Viktoria's section. Viktoria is a young attractive woman with long blonde hair, blue eyes, and a thick German accent.

HOSTESS (CONT'D)

Vik, you got a table hon

Viktoria looks at Alurich, and is stunned. He sits alone at the table. She quietly crosses to him.

VIKTORIA

Hello, how are you?

ALURICH

You are German

                    VIKTORIA

Yeah, you know what you want?

                    ALURICH

Yes, burnt toast, olives, and black coffee

                    VIKTORIA

I'll be right back with your order sir

Viktoria walks away.

INT. KITCHEN - NIGHT

Viktoria enters the kitchen and contacts her manager, Steve, who is standing in front of the cook's line wearing a blue suit.

                    VIKTORIA

        Steve

                    STEVE

Yeah, what is it?

                    VIKTORIA

That guy wants burnt toast

                    STEVE

He comes in here all the time, gets the same thing, black coffee, burnt toast, and olives, looks like the living dead, you know?

                    VIKTORIA

He asked to be seated in my section

                    STEVE

Sounds like you have an admirer. Order twelve, you're up!

                    VIKTORIA

I don't mind serving him. What number is he?

                     STEVE

Thirteen

INT. RESTAURANT - NIGHT

Viktoria hands Alurich his black plate and check.

                    VIKTORIA

How was everything?

                    ALURICH

I cannot accept this

                    VIKTORIA

What? Why?

                    ALURICH

This check is green; I am always given a black
one

                    VIKTORIA

What difference does it make what color your
check is?

                    ALURICH

I have an addiction to black

                    VIKTORIA

Here, use this

Viktoria hands Alurich a black magic marker.

ALURICH

Thank you

Alurich begins coloring the green check black. Viktoria looks at him
like he's crazy. Once Alurich is finished painting the green check
black he takes out black painted money and hands it to Viktoria.

VIKTORIA

I'll be back

INT. KITCHEN - NIGHT

Viktoria walks into the kitchen and places Alurich's money inside of
the register. She rips the paper from the printer and takes the receipt.

INT. RESTAURANT - NIGHT

Viktoria returns to Alurich's table. He is cleaning his own plastic
black fork and knife with a black painted sanitation wipe. A small
black box is sitting on the table.

VIKTORIA

Here you go sir. How was your meal?

ALURICH

Excellent

VIKTORIA

Good. Does the black paint have trouble
sticking?

ALURICH
(In relief)
Yes, it is nice to know that you care

VIKTORIA

Well, I wouldn't go that far. I hope you have a
wonderful night, please come back and see us

Viktoria walks away. Moments later Alurich stands up and walks
towards the front. Viktoria franticly runs towards Alurich with the
black box in her hand once he reaches the entrance doors.

VIKTORIA (CONT'D)

Sir! You forgot this

Viktoria hands Alurich the black box.

ALURICH

This is your tip

Alurich hands her back the box, and firmly holds her hand in solemn
importance.

ALURICH (CONT'D)

You need to promise me that you will take good
care of this because it is very important to us

VIKTORIA
(trying not to laugh)
...Ok

ALURICH

I will be over at your house on Friday night

VIKTORIA

I have to work Friday

ALURICH

We will go out and eat Saturday night

VIKTORIA

I have to work Saturday

ALURICH

I will be over at your house Monday night and
we will go out to dinner. I will arrange the
evening all expenses paid. We will enjoy our
time together

Alurich begins to exit the restaurant until his departure is interrupted.

VIKTORIA

How do you know where I live?

ALURICH
(With his back turned)
I know everything

Alurich exits the restaurant.

HOSTESS

Have a good night. What a freak. I think he's
stalking you. Are you going to go out with him?

VIKTORIA

Yes

HOSTESS

Freak! You're a freak!

VIKTORIA

I am not

HOSTESS

What's in the box?

INT. ALURICH'S CELL - NIGHT

Alurich opens his steel black oven door and grabs a glowing red hot steel pipe with his bare hand. He squeezes the pole tightly with his hand and doesn't have any reaction towards the poles heat. He places the steaming black pipe on a nearby black shelf once it is cooled. Alurich puts on a black dress shirt over his black T-shirt. He buttons the dress shirt and ties a black tie around the collar. He puts on a black vest over his dress shirt. He picks up thirteen white roses and spray paints each one completely black.

EXT. VIKTORIA'S MANSION - SUNSET

Viktoria's house is located in a rural setting surrounded by large evergreen trees and luscious green grass. The house is a Neoclassical Victorian white mansion. Alurich walks across the giant lawn and up the steps between the high white pillars. He reaches the double white doors with a bouquet of thirteen painted black roses. He knocks on the double white doors and Viktoria answers.

> ALURICH
> (Handing her the black roses)
> Here, these are for you

> VIKTORIA
> Thank you, please, come in

INT. VIKTORIA'S MANSION - SUNSET

Alurich enters Viktoria's mansion. She is wearing a tight white sweater with a white skirt and white shoes. Her long blonde hair and bright blue eyes shine. The inside of Viktoria's mansion is completely white and filled with gleaming light throughout. There is a spiraling white staircase to the right of the front double white doors. A white grand piano sits in the living room with a white sofa under the high vaulting white cathedral ceiling. The white mansion is decorated in lavish taste, and everything inside of the mansion is white. A boy dressed in gray walks across the white tiled floor and over to Viktoria.

VIKTORIA

Alurich, this is my son, Kerry. Kerry, introduce yourself to Alurich

KERRY

Hello

Alurich bends down to shake Kerry's hand and stares into Kerry's eyes. Alurich is bewildered by them, but doesn't show any emotion towards their familiarity.

ALURICH

Hello

Kerry takes off running into the living room.

VIKTORIA

Are you ready?

ALURICH

I am ready

INT. POOL HALL - NIGHT

Alurich and Viktoria are inside of a dark pool hall. Alurich has a black pool stick and Viktoria a white one. They play pool on a green pool table. They are the only people who are there. Viktoria breaks the balls and begins to clear the table.

VIKTORIA

It's nice you found such a private place

ALURICH

You like quiet places

VIKTORIA

Yes, I do, I guess it depends on my mood.
Sometimes I like loud places with many people.
Other times quiet, depends on the situation

ALURICH

It is difficult for me to play on this table

VIKTORIA

What? Why?

ALURICH

It is green

VIKTORIA

Yes, it is green, so?

ALURICH

Everything must be black, it is an addiction

VIKTORIA

Ok, whatever, I'm sure this must be killing you
then, what about the balls?

ALURICH

They are colorful

VIKTORIA

Maybe this can be a start of new colors for you

ALURICH

You are good

VIKTORIA

Who? Me? Nah, I'm not that good

ALURICH

You have not missed

Viktoria continues to knock the balls into all of the pockets.

ALURICH (CONT'D)

I never asked your last name

VIKTORIA

Von Buren, and you?

ALURICH

Korall

VIKTORIA

Tell me about yourself

ALURICH

Why are you here?

VIKTORIA

Usually a question isn't answered with another one. Why am I here? My family died and I was left an inheritance. You?

ALURICH

There is a lot

VIKTORIA

We have a lot of time, any family?

ALURICH

No family, no friends

VIKTORIA

I am here with you right now

ALURICH

Everyone and everything died from the war

VIKTORIA

It sounds like we have something in common

ALURICH

We do, you have a son, where is the father?

VIKTORIA

My son's father died in the war

Viktoria knocks in the final ball with her white pool stick.

VIKTORIA (CONT'D)

I win

ALURICH

Would you like to play again?

VIKTORIA

You must really like to lose

ALURICH

There is not a preference

VIKTORIA

Losers rack

Alurich begins loading the balls into the rack.

ALURICH

I hope you realize this is very difficult for me

VIKTORIA

All of those colors, it must be

ALURICH

You enjoy torturing me

VIKTORIA

You enjoy torturing yourself

ALURICH

I do

Alurich finishes racking the balls and Viktoria breaks them with her white pool stick.

ALURICH (CONT'D)

So what sort of things do you enjoy?

VIKTORIA

Pool

ALURICH

Besides pool

VIKTORIA

I like pretty pictures and the unusual

ALURICH

You must like me then. Pictures are depressing

VIKTORIA

Is that because all the pictures you see people are sad, or angry?

ALURICH

Could be, is there anyplace you would like to go
after this? I am your chauffeur this evening

VIKTORIA

I don't care

ALURICH

We can eat, but only where you work

VIKTORIA

Why where I work?

ALURICH

It is the only place with black tables and chairs,
black menus, they burn my food. I can handle
it

VIKTORIA

Can you handle it? That's good

Viktoria hits the eight ball really hard with the cue ball. The eight
ball flies off of the table towards Alurich at a blistering speed and he
catches it.

VIKTORIA (CONT'D)

Nice catch

INT. ALURICH'S CELL - NIGHT

Alurich and Viktoria enter Alurich's cell.

VIKTORIA

This is where you live? Nice view

ALURICH

The skyscrapers look like gravestones from down here

VIKTORIA

It's freezing

ALURICH

No heat, no pain

Viktoria takes the whip off of the wall.

VIKTORIA

What are you into?

ALURICH

That is something that is not right

Viktoria puts the whip back on the wall.

VIKTORIA

Ok, this is brutal, what a grand piano, I love the piano, can you play?

ALURICH

Yes, excuse me

Alurich enters the bathroom. Viktoria continues to tap on the black piano keys.

INT. ALURICH'S BATHROOM - NIGHT

Alurich takes a knife out of the cabinet and slices his hand open with it. He sews his hand up with black thread and a needle while the blood trickles down his palm, wrist, and arm.

INT. ALURICH'S CELL - NIGHT

Viktoria lifts the black sheet from the corner of Alurich's bed and accidently pokes the tip of her finger with a nail. She turns around and Alurich surprisingly grabs her hand and startles her.

> ALURICH

Just common curiosity

> VIKTORIA

I have to go

> ALURICH

You are bleeding

Viktoria begins sucking on her finger

> VIKTORIA

Oh no, I'm ok, really, it's not bad. I have to be up early, but it was really nice meeting you

> ALURICH

You like blood. I have grown to like my own. It is black

> VIKTORIA

What? No, I don't like blood, I'm ok, I mean it

> ALURICH

Be careful on your way home. There can be a lot of real scaries out this time of night. Do you need a walk?

> VIKTORIA

I know, I will, goodbye. Have a good night

Viktoria quickly exits the cell up the stairs.

ALURICH

Game over

Alurich walks over to his bed, swipes the black sheet from the top, and reveals a bed of nails.

EXT. STONE ROCK HOUSE - DAY

Viktoria is wearing all white as she walks through the desolate area near the lake. She enters the small stone rock house.

INT. RED ROOM - DAY

Viktoria enters the dimly lit red room and takes a seat in a black chair located in the middle of the room. A man's deep voice comes out through the speakers.

MAN'S VOICE

What brings you here today?

VIKTORIA

I have many questions about him

INT. BLACK ROOM - DAY

CLOSE-UP: KERRY'S MOUTH

KERRY

And you come to me? Why not...

INT. RED ROOM - DAY

MAN'S VOICE

Ask him?

VIKTORIA

I want the truth

INT. BLACK ROOM - DAY

CLOSE-UP: KERRY'S MOUTH

KERRY

What makes you think I know?

Viktoria's voice is heard through the intercom.

VIKTORIA

Because you do

KERRY

Alurich was part of a psychological experiment
conducted during the war

INT. RED ROOM - NIGHT

The man's voice is heard coming through the speakers. Viktoria
continues to sit in the black chair in the middle of the room.

MAN'S VOICE

He was a prisoner held captive along with his
wife at a concentration camp. The black coats
attempted to condition him through the source
of habit, their goal...pain

VIKTORIA

What about his obsession with black?

INT. BLACK ROOM - NIGHT

CLOSE UP: KERRY'S MOUTH

> KERRY
>
> He was blindfolded at all times, trained to dull
> his...

INT. RED ROOM - NIGHT

The man's voice comes through the speakers. Viktoria continues to sit in the black chair in the middle of the red room.

> MAN'S VOICE
>
> Senses

> VIKTORIA
>
> Why does he mutilate himself?

INT. BLACK ROOM - NIGHT

CLOSE UP: KERRY'S MOUTH

> KERRY
>
> Why would anyone?

Viktoria's voice is heard through the intercom.

> VIKTORIA
>
> Attention? Expression? I don't know

INT. RED ROOM - NIGHT

Viktoria sits in the middle of the red room on a black chair. The man's voice comes through the speakers.

                    MAN'S VOICE

    You are right for the most part. He inflicts
    physical pain

                    VIKTORIA

    That's impossible. No person can withstand
    such punishment

                    MAN'S VOICE

    That's why it is unique. His compulsion is
    uncanny

INT. BLACK ROOM - NIGHT

CLOSE-UP: KERRY'S MOUTH

                    KERRY

    He is completely indifferent

INT. RED ROOM - NIGHT

                    VIKTORIA

    I went to his home. He lives underground in a
    cement cell. It was freezing. He sleeps on a bed
    of nails

                    MAN'S VOICE

    Well that's not surprising. He was forced to live
    in such a place during that time in his life, to
    sleep...

INT. BLACK ROOM - NIGHT

CLOSE UP: KERRY'S MOUTH

                    KERRY

        On shattered glass. He has been so well trained
        that he does everything to the same identity

INT. RED ROOM - NIGHT

                    VIKTORIA

        He enjoys it?

                    MAN'S VOICE

        No

INT. BLACK ROOM - NIGHT

CLOSE UP: KERRY'S MOUTH

                    KERRY

        It is an addiction. He inflicts damage and heals.
        Where are you taking off to?

INT. RED ROOM - NIGHT

Viktoria stands up and begins to exit the red room.

                    VIKTORIA

        I am leaving, thank you for your time

                    MAN'S VOICE

        Before you go...

INT. BLACK ROOM - NIGHT

CLOSE UP: KERRY'S MOUTH

KERRY

It is important that you understand that he
is not dangerous physically, only to himself,
but not to be provoked. Be sensitive to his
instability

INT. RED ROOM - NIGHT

VIKTORIA

I'll keep that in mind

Viktoria exits the red room.

INT. ALURICH'S CELL - NIGHT

Viktoria enters Alurich's cell. She is wearing all white clothing and
he is wearing all black, but doesn't have his face painted. Alurich
is playing "Moonlight Sonata" on the black piano, and his back is
turned to Viktoria. He doesn't have any idea that she is in the cell.
He finishes playing, turns around, and notices that she is standing
there. Alurich stands and Viktoria walks over to him. She gives him
a hug.

VIKTORIA

How long has it been since you held someone in
your arms?

Alurich doesn't say anything.

VIKTORIA (CONT'D)

You play beautifully; you should come to the church and play

ALURICH

For me, it is not right

VIKTORIA

They have a giant black organ with big black pedals

ALURICH

Are the keys black?

VIKTORIA

I...I don't know

Alurich is silent.

VIKTORIA (CONT'D)

The bibles are black

Alurich gives her a sardonic stare.

INT. CHURCH - MORNING

CLOSE UP: CRUCIFIXION

FADE TO:

The scene begins with a close up on the face of a white statue of Jesus. The camera fades back and reveals a giant white Jesus on a large black cross hanging from the ceiling of the church in the back of the altar. The church is half-filled with the elderly and families sitting throughout. The interior color combination is completely black and white with dim yellow lighting. The Minister takes the podium.

MINISTER

Hello everyone, welcome to our Sunday service.
It is wonderful to have all of you with us here on
this rainy morning. We will begin our day with
a special guest. Alurich Korall will be joining us
with a recital. Where is Alurich?

INT. CHURCH ENTRANCE ROOM -
MORNING

Alurich stands and waits in the pitch black church entrance room in
front of the large black wooden double doors. He opens the enlarged
doors and the yellow light from the church cathedral shines in
brightly. He walks into the cathedral.

INT. CHURCH - MORNING

Alurich walks down the church hall and everyone stares at him. He
is dressed in an all black suit, and his face is painted white as always.
He walks up to the organ and takes a seat in front of it. He begins
playing 'Toccata & Fugue in D minor'. The audience is both shocked
and terrified. The camera displays all of the different facial reactions
of the people in the church. First, an indifferent old man is shown.
Second, a young woman covers her ears in disgust. Third, a smiling
young man displays happiness. Fourth, an elderly woman covers her
mouth in shock. Fifth, a little girl covers her eyes in fear. Sixth, a
young woman frowns with sadness. These shots show the irony of
emotion others have when Alurich plays the organ perfectly and with
indifference. Alurich finishes playing the piece and takes a seat next
to Viktoria.

MINISTER

That was...very good

INT. CHURCH - DAY

The people are in a single file line waiting to shake hands with the minister. Viktoria shakes the minister's hand.

MINISTER

Hello Viktoria, I'm glad you could make it.
Hello Alurich, that was an interesting recital

Alurich and the Minister shake hands. Alurich is wearing black gloves.

CLOSE UP: ALURICH'S BLACK HAND AND MINISTER'S WHITE HAND EMBRACING

ALURICH

You can thank your lord that it was raining this morning or else I would not have been here

VIKTORIA

He has issues with sunlight

MINISTER

Thank you for joining us

VIKTORIA

Thank you

MINISTER

I hope to see you again

VIKTORIA

You will

Alurich and Viktoria exit the church.

EXT. STONE ROCK HOUSE - DAY

Alurich enters the desolate stone rock house on a rainy day. He is dressed in complete black and face is painted white as always.

INT. RED ROOM - DAY

Alurich enters the dim red room and takes a seat in a white chair. The soft woman's voice comes in through the black speakers.

> WOMAN'S VOICE
> Hello, have a seat. How have you been?

> ALURICH
> Jagged, cold and numb

> WOMAN'S VOICE
> You look better

INT. BLACK ROOM - DAY

Kerry sits alone in the black room.

CLOSE UP: KERRY'S MOUTH

> KERRY
> What is bothering you?

INT. RED ROOM - DAY

> ALURICH
> Viktoria, there is something vaguely familiar
> about her son

INT. BLACK ROOM - DAY

CLOSE UP: KERRY'S MOUTH

                    KERRY
          Some of us are just familiar

INT. RED ROOM - DAY

                    ALURICH
          When I looked into his eyes there was
          something chilling about them. I felt a feeling I
          have not felt since...

INT. BLACK ROOM - DAY

                    KERRY
          Since when?

INT. RED ROOM - DAY

                    ALURICH
          Since I was a prisoner

                    WOMAN'S VOICE
          That is interesting. Do you plan to continue
          seeing her?

                    ALURICH
          Yes

                    WOMAN'S VOICE
          I have seen her too

                          ALURICH

You have?

INT. BLACK ROOM - DAY

CLOSE UP: KERRY'S MOUTH

                           KERRY

Yes, I told her everything. Is that ok with you?

Alurich's voice is heard through the intercom.

                          ALURICH

It is

INT. RED ROOM - DAY

Alurich begins to exit the red room, but is interrupted.

                     WOMAN'S VOICE

I couldn't help to notice something about
Viktoria

Alurich stops at the door.

INT. BLACK ROOM - DAY

CLOSE UP: KERRY'S MOUTH

                           KERRY

She was wearing white, why would someone

who obsessively commits himself to black be
infatuated with a woman who...

INT. RED ROOM - DAY

WOMAN'S VOICE

Is surrounded completely by white?

CLOSE UP: ALURICH'S FACE

ALURICH

Black on black gives me a heart attack

Alurich exits the red room.

EXT. HAUNTED HOUSE - NIGHT

Viktoria and Alurich wait in line outside a haunted house on
Halloween night. Viktoria is dressed in white and Alurich is dressed
in complete black with his painted white face. Everyone among them
is dressed in Halloween costumes. A vampire approaches Alurich.

VAMPIRE

Hey! You need to get back in there. The other
two vampires are on break and we need more
for the dragon pit

ALURICH

I do not work here

VAMPIRE

Oh, my bad, the costume confused me

ALURICH

This is not a costume and I am not a vampire

VAMPIRE

Yeah, whatever, see you around man

Viktoria and Alurich reach the ticket booth. There is a woman dressed like a witch standing behind the booth.

WITCH

Ok, how many?

ALURICH

Two

Alurich hands her painted black money and the witch hands Viktoria the white tickets.

WITCH

Follow Shantay, the goddess of darkness

SHANTAY

Hello, I am Shantay, the goddess of darkness, follow me into the lair of hell if you dare, but remember, once you go in, you may never come back out

Everyone standing in the crowd follows her into the Haunted House.

INT. BUTCHER'S ROOM - NIGHT

Alurich and Viktoria walk into a dark butcher's room along with the crowd. Alurich and Viktoria stand in front of the insane bloody butcher as he slices a dead body lying on an operating table.

BUTCHER

Hello my yummy friends. It looks like we have some fresh flesh in here tonight, just perfect for my cleaver! So which one of ya want to be first?

All of the children jump back in fright.

ALURICH

You should not use a cleaver to cut skin, a sharp
knife works best

BUTCHER

Oh, and what do you know about cutting
human flesh?

Alurich unbuttons his shirt and shows the Butcher his cut and burn
marks. The Butcher drops his cleaver in shock.

BUTCHER (CONT'D)

What the hell?

The crowd exits the butcher's room.

INT. CEMETERY ROOM - NIGHT

Alurich and Viktoria enter the cemetery room along with everyone
else. The room is decorated with tombstones, skeletons, cobwebs,
and smog. A zombie directs the line of people.

ZOMBIE

Ok, everyone go through this hole one at a
time, watch your heads

One by one the people enter the hole and fall down a slide that leads
outside. Loud screams and the sound of chain-saws are heard coming
from the outside. Alurich and Viktoria enter the black hole.

EXT. HAUNTED HOUSE - NIGHT

Viktoria and Alurich slide down the black hole and depart out the
Haunted House exterior wall. Alurich descends through the outer

hole first and Viktoria follows. Men in ski masks chase screaming children around with chain-saws.

> VIKTORIA
>
> Wow, I haven't been to a haunted house since I was little. This is so much fun! Those guys are chasing those poor kids must be terrified. Is that it?

> ALURICH
>
> Yeah, are you ready?

INT. VIKTORIA'S MANSION - NIGHT

Alurich and Viktoria enter the white mansion.

> VIKTORIA
>
> You can have a seat

Viktoria walks up the spiraling white staircase.

MEDIUM SHOT: ALURICH STANDING
ALONE IN HER WHITE MANSION

FULL BODY SHOT: ALURICH STANDING
ALONE IN HER WHITE MANSION

BIRD'S EYE VIEW: ALURICH STANDING
ALONE IN HER WHITE MANSION

The purpose of these shots is to show Alurich progressively becoming a distant small trace of black alone in a world of white. Each shot directly follows one after another. He walks into the spacious living room and sits on the white love seat. Viktoria enters.

INT. VIKTORIA'S LIVING ROOM - NIGHT

The living room is entirely white. Viktoria takes a seat next to Alurich.

VIKTORIA

Alurich, I wanted us to be alone tonight.
There's something I've needed to tell you

ALURICH

What is it?

VIKTORIA

I know that you were a prisoner during the war.
My family were members of the Black Coats

ALURICH

Everyone was a member then. There was only
a small majority that had a choice. Where are
they now?

VIKTORIA

Everyone is dead. They died during the
bombing of our city. I was lucky enough not
to be there at the time of the bombing. My
life was spared and I was left a large inheritance
from my family. That's how I got this place

ALURICH

Good for you

VIKTORIA

I know what happened to you and I feel guilty.
I'm sorry Alurich

ALURICH

I am not offended

VIKTORIA

Good

ALURICH

Your husband, what happened to him?

VIKTORIA

My husband was a soldier that died during the war. We were married for thirteen years

ALURICH

You married young

VIKTORIA

I was very young. He was the only man I ever loved. I had never met somebody with so much charm and love in them. Nobody has ever made me feel the way he did

ALURICH

Well, I still have time

VIKTORIA

I was pregnant with Kerry while he was off for duty with the Black Coats. He never had the chance to meet his son

ALURICH

That is unfortunate. How did he die?

VIKTORIA

They found him dead on the battlefield. I have a picture of him

Viktoria walks over to the white bookcase and pulls a picture out of the drawer. She carries it to Alurich and hands it to him.

> VIKTORIA (CONT'D)
>
> Here, this is him

Alurich looks at the picture of her husband's face. The man's face is Colonel Hugo K. Snyder.

> VIKTORIA (CONT'D)
>
> I gave him a watch before he went off to war to remember me by. It was a black lacquer pocket watch with a Tao on the head of it. It's said that the yang represents the light, active, positive principle, and the yin represents the dark, passive negativity. They say that life would be impossible without both energies and it illustrates unity. It had been in my family for years. I thought it would give him optimism in such a difficult time. He told me that he would always carry it with him, but it was gone when they found him dead

Alurich covers Snyder's face with his hand and stands.

> ALURICH
>
> That is quite a story

Alurich hands the picture of Snyder back to Viktoria.

> ALURICH (CONT'D)
>
> I have to go

> VIKTORIA
>
> What? Why are you leaving? Are you ok?

ALURICH

No, I am not

VIKTORIA

What's wrong?

ALURICH

I have a few things that I need to do

VIKTORIA

(Sarcastically)

What? Do you have to go mutilate yourself
again?

ALURICH

That was unnecessary

VIKTORIA

I'm sorry, I was joking

ALURICH

I will see you in a while, goodbye

Alurich exits Viktoria's mansion. Viktoria is left confused.

INT. ALURICH'S BATHROOM - NIGHT

Alurich is standing in front of his bathroom mirror with the left side
of his face painted white and the right side of his face painted black.
He is wearing a black shirt.

ALURICH

Now we know who he is, and this ground is not
the rock we thought it would be

Alurich covers the white side of his face with his hand, and leaves the black side uncovered.

ALURICH (CONT'D)

I can kill him

Alurich switches hands and covers the black side of his face and leaves the white side uncovered.

ALURICH (CONT'D)

He is just a boy

Alurich covers the white side of his face with his hand, and leaves the black side uncovered.

ALURICH (CONT'D)

The sons' of Kane do not receive reprieve

Alurich switches hands and covers the black side of his face and leaves the white side uncovered.

ALURICH (CONT'D)

He is not him

Alurich covers the white side of his face with his hand, and leaves the black side uncovered.

ALURICH (CONT'D)

But there is one in the other

Alurich switches hands and covers the black side of his face and leaves the white side uncovered.

ALURICH (CONT'D)

Not with the other, you will be haunted

Alurich covers the white side of his face with his hand, and leaves the black side uncovered.

ALURICH (CONT'D)

We are already haunted

Alurich switches hands and covers the black side of his face and leaves the white side uncovered.

ALURICH (CONT'D)

She can end that, and forgive you, but if you kill
him you will always be haunted and forsaken

Alurich covers the white side of his face with his hand, and leaves the black side uncovered.

ALURICH (CONT'D)

You already are

Alurich switches hands and covers the black side of his face and leaves the white side uncovered.

ALURICH (CONT'D)

It will be a new beginning

Alurich covers the white side of his face with his hand, and leaves the black side uncovered.

ALURICH (CONT'D)

It will be a new beginning any ways, kill him

Alurich switches hands and covers the black side of his face and leaves the white side uncovered.

ALURICH (CONT'D)

That is unnecessary

Alurich covers the white side of his face with his hand, and leaves the black side uncovered.

ALURICH (CONT'D)

The truth will hurt her

Alurich switches hands and covers the black side of his face and leaves the white side uncovered.

ALURICH (CONT'D)

The truth is necessary for growth

Alurich covers the white side of his face with his hand, and leaves the black side uncovered.

ALURICH (CONT'D)

She does not need to know

Alurich switches hands and covers the black side of his face and leaves the white side uncovered.

ALURICH (CONT'D)

It is the right thing to do

Alurich covers the white side of his face with his hand, and leaves the black side uncovered.

ALURICH (CONT'D)

She does not love you

Alurich switches hands and covers the black side of his face and leaves the white side uncovered.

ALURICH (CONT'D)

She can love me if I get rid of you

Alurich covers the white side of his face with his hand, and leaves the black side uncovered.

ALURICH (CONT'D)

I am what attracted her

Alurich switches hands and covers the black side of his face and leaves the white side uncovered.

ALURICH (CONT'D)

That is false

Alurich covers the white side of his face with his hand, and leaves the black side uncovered.

ALURICH (CONT'D)

How could she love someone like you?

Alurich switches hands and covers the black side of his face and leaves the white side uncovered.

ALURICH (CONT'D)

She loved Snyder

Alurich covers the white side of his face with his hand, and leaves the black side uncovered.

ALURICH (CONT'D)

Snyder, I killed him now I have become him

Alurich switches hands and covers the black side of his face and leaves the white side uncovered.

ALURICH (CONT'D)

You are not him

Alurich covers the white side of his face with his hand, and leaves the black side uncovered.

ALURICH (CONT'D)

If you are not him, then who is me?

Alurich switches hands and covers the black side of his face and leaves the white side uncovered.

ALURICH (CONT'D)

I am I

Alurich puts his hand down and leaves his entire face, both black and white sides open.

ALURICH (CONT'D)

She loves both of us or neither of us. There is
not one without the other. Nobody is perfect.
Her mystery is her darkness

EXT. PARK - NIGHT

Alurich and Viktoria are on a chariot ride through the park on a cold autumn night. Alurich is dressed in black with his face painted in white makeup and Viktoria is dressed in white as always. They sit in a black carriage and two white horses pull them forward. A man dressed in a brown suit directs the horses in front of them.

VIKTORIA

It's cold out tonight. Aren't you cold?

Alurich doesn't say anything.

VIKTORIA (CONT'D)

Oh, I forgot you don't have any feeling

Alurich hands Viktoria a small black and white photograph of Freya.

VIKTORIA (CONT'D)

Who is this?

ALURICH

Freya, my dead wife

VIKTORIA

Oh, so this is Freya. She's beautiful, what happened to her?

ALURICH

She was murdered

VIKTORIA

That's terrible. Did they ever find who did it?

ALURICH

They have a hunch

VIKTORIA

Good, I believe all who are guilty should be incarcerated

ALURICH

As do I

VIKTORIA

The same thing happened to me so I know what it's like. I know what it's like to lose someone

ALURICH

I know you do

INT. ALURICH'S CELL - NIGHT

Alurich and Viktoria enter the cell.

VIKTORIA

I don't know why we come to your place. It's
freezing out tonight and you live without heat...
which is insane

ALURICH

No heat, no...

VIKTORIA

(Interrupting)
Yes, I know, no pain, very good, let's go to my
place

ALURICH

Do you not like it here?

VIKTORIA

Alurich! Of course I like it here, your place is
really different, but come on

Alurich walks into the bathroom and washes the white paint off his
face. He returns to Viktoria without any white paint on his face.

ALURICH

Viktoria, there is something I need to tell you

VIKTORIA

What?

ALURICH

(Startled)
Oh my, that is the first time I have used cold
water in a long time

VIKTORIA

...Ok, are you awake now?

ALURICH

How could everything I fear become everything I enjoy, and everything I desire become everything I loathe?

VIKTORIA

I don't know; you ready?

ALURICH

I need to know why you love me

VIKTORIA

I never said I did, but you can't help what you feel. Are you in love with me?

ALURICH

I do not believe in love

VIKTORIA

You lie

ALURICH

How could you have loved him?

VIKTORIA

Who?

ALURICH

Snyder

VIKTORIA

How do you know my ex-husband's last name? I never told you. Not that it's important; I had

my last name changed back to my maiden after
he died. I thought it would help me move on

ALURICH

Because I killed him

VIKTORIA

What do you mean you killed him? He died on
the battlefield

ALURICH

Your husband was commandant of the camp I
was being held at

VIKTORIA

My husband was the leader of an infantry unit
responsible for attacking the eastern alliance.
He was never at a camp

ALURICH

Viktoria, listen to me, your husband was
responsible for thousands of deaths, he
conducted the experiments; he marched over
a hundred people to a remote area and buried
them alive. I was buried along with my wife. I
clawed my way out of the ground and trekked
back to the camp in the sleeting ice and snow

VIKTORIA

Wow, sounds like you had a pretty tough time
there. I understand that you have a somewhat
dark sense of humor Alurich, but this is much
by even your standards

ALURICH

This is not a joke. Everything that you have been told is a lie. It is not surprising. The politicians have lied to everyone in order to cover the past. You were one of them. I was one of them

VIKTORIA

Ok, fine, you killed my husband, Colonel Hugo K. Snyder. You killed him. You say that he tortured you in his camp of concentration worse than any animal and marched you out to the middle of nowhere and buried you alive along with your wife. You clawed your way out of the ground and went back to the camp determined to get a mark of revenge on him. Ok, I believe you, but tell me this. If this crazy story of yours is indeed true, then where is your proof?

ALURICH

The box

VIKTORIA

What about it?

ALURICH

Do you have it with you?

Viktoria takes the black box out of her white purse.

VIKTORIA

You told me to bring it. Why would you leave me this as a tip? What is this?

ALURICH

Have you opened it?

VIKTORIA

What? No! What does this stupid box have to
do with anything?

ALURICH

Open it

VIKTORIA

It's locked

Alurich hands Viktoria a key. She opens the box and pulls out the
black lacquer pocket watch with the Tao on the head. She opens the
watch and it plays chimes. She looks at the inside and checks the
carved initials along with the dated black and white picture of herself.
She is speechless and shakes fiercely. She begins to cry in disbelief.

ALURICH

The denial

Viktoria slaps Alurich across the face with disgust as hard as she
possibly can. Alurich doesn't flinch and stands motionless. A black
tear rolls down his face from his eye. Viktoria sadly exits the cell.

INT. VIKTORIA'S MANSION - NIGHT

Viktoria is wearing all white. She enters her mansion and walks
into the living room. She sits on the love seat and Kerry enters. He
carries a small white wooden heart that has black pegs sticking out of
it. He is wearing red pajamas.

KERRY

Look at what I made at school today

VIKTORIA

What is it?

KERRY

It's a game

VIKTORIA

Well, how do you play?

KERRY

You skip peg by peg, see? The object of the
game is to have only one peg left; then you're a
genius

VIKTORIA

A genius? Have you played?

KERRY

Yeah, I always win. Here, try, I made it for you

VIKTORIA

This is a very thoughtful gift, thank you.
Kerry...

KERRY

Why don't you play?

VIKTORIA

I'll play later

KERRY

Here, play the game, you see? It's easy...

VIKTORIA

We need to talk

KERRY

About? What's wrong?

VIKTORIA

How do you feel about him?

KERRY

Who?

VIKTORIA

You know who

KERRY

...Is he my father?

VIKTORIA

You know he's not

KERRY

Are you sure about that?

VIKTORIA

Your father is dead, he died during the war; I let you know this a long time ago. I need to know how you feel about *him*

KERRY

You love him

VIKTORIA

Love is unrealistic

KERRY

You're only saying that because he killed my father

VIKTORIA

How do you know?

KERRY

I have spoken with him

VIKTORIA

Kerry, you need to keep your telepathy out of this. I am talking to *you*, the person, the child, my son, even if you know everything because of your psychic gift, I need to know how *you* feel

KERRY

I do not feel, how can you ask that of me when you know I'm telepathic

VIKTORIA

You are my son, please do not speak to me that way, I will send you on your way and nothing will ever change for any of us

KERRY

You have the power to do that, if it is what you want, you can ruin lives if it gives you joy

VIKTORIA

Kerry! Please...stop!

KERRY

That's impressive, most mothers would have just slapped their sons over egotism, but not you, that shows that you're good, and only good mothers will allow their children to have a joyous future

VIKTORIA

Ok, are you done? I speak to you like a person despite your ability, stop it. Stop it now

KERRY

I'm sorry, my apologies, I have a brilliant mind, but you already know that so there isn't any need for you to acknowledge it, so I'll stop

VIKTORIA

Don't act that way. You know better. That's why I trust in you. I know how difficult it must be with your abilities. How do you *feel*?

KERRY

(Crying)
Why do you ask!? I don't know!

VIKTORIA

Kerry, come on, this is necessary, relax

KERRY

Don't you know that you can change him? So if you love him, what is stopping you?

VIKTORIA

He should change himself

KERRY

Nobody is perfect. That is a contradiction

VIKTORIA

I need to know if you love him

KERRY

You're asking too much!

VIKTORIA

Kerry, please, relax, I don't want to pressure you,
ok? You have a gift. Your telepathy gives you
the ability to know what others are thinking,
and what they want, or ask of you. That's why
I need to know, because your judgment as my
son holds the most credibility considering your
position on this matter. So...do you love him?

KERRY

He is a part of me...like my father. He killed
him...now he has become him, but he isn't a
good man without you. That is his allegory.
Neither was my father, so therefore my love for
him cannot exist without your love for him

Kerry walks up the spiraling white staircase, enters his bedroom, and
shuts the door. Viktoria takes her picture of Snyder out of the drawer
and burns it.

INT. ALURICH'S CELL - NIGHT

Viktoria enters the cell. She is wearing all white. Alurich is lying on
his back on the bed of nails with glowing scorpions crawling all over
his chest in the dark.

VIKTORIA

The scorpions are ultra-fluorescent because the
hyaline in their exoskeleton contains protein

Viktoria turns on the dim yellow lights.

VIKTORIA (CONT'D)

That's why they glow in the dark

ALURICH

You have come back. It has been thirteen days
since I last saw you. I did not know if you
would be back

VIKTORIA

I am back...back to settle this

ALURICH

I like you

VIKTORIA

How can that honestly be possible Alurich?
You don't like anything. You don't like me.
You don't even like yourself. You go into the
bathroom and mutilate yourself instead of being
out here with me, how do you expect me to
believe that?

ALURICH

It is a sickness, but since meeting you I am
getting better

VIKTORIA

I know, and you will continue to get better even
without me

ALURICH

Are you leaving?

VIKTORIA

I never said that

ALURICH

Then what are you saying?

VIKTORIA

I'm saying that you need to live

ALURICH

They say that in order to become a saint one must go through hell first. I have been there, and I have to say that you are the closest thing to a saint I have ever met

VIKTORIA

I am not a saint. Nobody can be compared to Christ

ALURICH

Even Christ expressed his bitterness with man. So what makes us pure? What we feel or what we do?

VIKTORIA

Actions speak louder than words

ALURICH

So what is your reaction?

VIKTORIA

I need to know what it was like

ALURICH

So you want to be a saint. I will tell you what it was like. It was cold. It was very cold

VIKTORIA

What was he like?

ALURICH

He was cold as well

VIKTORIA

Despite what you say the man I knew was a
gentle, loving, caring person

ALURICH

He was a murderer!

VIKTORIA

Did he have a choice?

ALURICH

We always have a choice. I have killed men,
many men, and I am not saying that I did not
enjoy it, but that does not make it right

VIKTORIA

You don't make me feel good

ALURICH

Then why are you here?

VIKTORIA

Because I need this to end

ALURICH
(Shouting)
There is never an end! There is one life, and
only one! And it will continue even if you are

miserable! There can never be an end if there is not any means to justify it by! Once you die... you die; that's it!

VIKTORIA

Do you believe in means behind suicide?

ALURICH

Yes, but I would never, I do not want pain, I just need it to show that I am alive

VIKTORIA

Thank you

ALURICH

What

VIKTORIA

Thank you for finally expressing emotion

ALURICH

Are you lonely?

VIKTORIA

Yes, I am

ALURICH

Do you love me?

VIKTORIA
(Crying)
I don't want to hurt you

ALURICH

Vik, I have been cut, burned, beaten, stabbed, whipped, shot, scarred, frozen, and buried alive.

Only your reluctance will hurt me. Do not hold back

VIKTORIA

I'm not holding anything back, but I don't believe in love

ALURICH

Then what do we have?

VIKTORIA

I can't put a definition on it

ALURICH

You are reluctant

VIKTORIA

Things are not all black and white Alurich

ALURICH

So you have changed

VIKTORIA

Everything is constantly changing. You can't execute those who aren't what you want them to be, and if everyone was aware of that then none of this would have ever happened

ALURICH

Is your animosity for me so great that you would be willing to die for it?

VIKTORIA

One again you're being inaccurate, I never said I didn't love you

ALURICH
(Shouting)
Then what are you saying?!!

VIKTORIA
(Shouting)
Let go! Just let it go Alurich! It's not about
love! It's not about pride! It's not about the
past! It's about here! Now! Enjoy yourself
please! Life isn't a mystery for you to figure out!
It's an adventure to be lived! Let it go!

ALURICH
(Smiling)
I love you

VIKTORIA
Ok, I love you too

ALURICH
What about your son?

VIKTORIA
Let's not bring him into this

ALURICH
He is what led me to you

VIKTORIA
His telepathy is unexplained, but that still
doesn't mean that he is only a boy despite his
gift

ALURICH
He speaks to me on another level of

consciousness. That is how I knew what I did.
He is the one who brought us together

VIKTORIA

I know he is, the same happened to me

ALURICH

Does he have the strength to accept me despite
my past with his father?

VIKTORIA

How strong do we need to be in order to be
loved? Your past with Snyder is an issue, but
doesn't have an affect on his brilliance

ALURICH

None of this can be explained

VIKTORIA

That doesn't matter

ALURICH

Have you ever made love on a bed of nails?

VIKTORIA

No

ALURICH

Would you like to?

VIKTORIA

Only if I get to be on top

ALURICH

I wouldn't have it any other way

VIKTORIA

The things I do for you

Viktoria and Alurich begin kissing. They slowly undress each other and get on top of the bed of nails Viktoria gets on top of Alurich and they cover themselves under a black sheet. They roll around on the bed of nails in ecstasy without pain as they make love together.

EXT. STONE ROCK HOUSE - DAY

Alurich strolls down the path leading to the desolate house by the lake on a sunny day. He is dressed in black and wearing sunglasses without any white paint on his bare face.

INT. RED ROOM - DAY

Alurich takes a seat in the white chair located in the middle of the room. He removes his sunglasses as the soft woman's voice speaks through the black speakers.

WOMAN'S VOICE

It's sunny out, what are you doing here?

ALURICH

I have began to go outside during the day now
when the sun is out, but must wear sunglasses so
the light does not blind me

WOMAN'S VOICE

Why the sudden change?

ALURICH

Black and white are all I saw in my past, red and
yellow then came to be, reaching out...let's me
see

INT. BLACK ROOM - DAY

Kerry sits in the black room by himself and speaks into the microphone.

CLOSE UP: KERRY'S MOUTH

KERRY

Tell me about the trauma

Alurich's voice comes through the intercom.

ALURICH

I was frozen, and could not feel anything. I was covered by dirt and trapped under a layer of ice

KERRY

How did you...

INT. RED ROOM - DAY

WOMAN'S VOICE

Get out?

ALURICH

I busted through the ice with my hands and clawed my way out of the ground. These people had the ability to kill with such a lack of compassion. They killed...without meaning, without reason. They killed for the pure enjoyment of killing. And their victims went without retention, without regret. They were like the lamb being led to the slaughter. It was as if history had already written itself

INT. BLACK ROOM - DAY

CLOSE UP: KERRY'S MOUTH

> KERRY
>
> Do you miss her?

Alurich's voice comes in through the intercom.

> ALURICH
>
> We loved a lifetime's worth

> KERRY
>
> You are in love with your own…

INT. RED ROOM - DAY

> WOMAN'S VOICE
>
> Misery?

> ALURICH
>
> Not anymore

> WOMAN'S VOICE
>
> How do you feel after confronting all of this?

> ALURICH
>
> It is as it was

INT. BLACK ROOM - DAY

CLOSE UP: KERRY'S MOUTH

KERRY

How do you feel about her?

Alurich's voice is heard through the intercom.

ALURICH

It feels good to have a friend

KERRY

You know Alurich...

INT. RED ROOM - DAY

Alurich begins to exit the red room. He is standing by the door before he is interrupted.

WOMAN'S VOICE

I wasn't the one who saved you

ALURICH
(Laughing)
Who are you?

WOMAN'S VOICE

Why do you ask questions you already know the answers to?

INT. BLACK ROOM - DAY

CLOSE UP: KERRY'S MOUTH

KERRY

You don't need me for that when you obviously know who I am

INT. RED ROOM - DAY

ALURICH

I will see you soon my son

Alurich exits the red room.

FADE TO BLACK.

REMISSION

TITLE CARD:

'REMISSION'

FADE IN:

EXT. VIKTORIA'S MANSION - DAY

'REMISSION' is shot in color. We PAN across a gray sky and reveal Viktoria's white mansion. The rain is pouring and Alurich is playing his black grand piano in front of her mansion in the middle of the massive green lawn. He is dressed in a white collared shirt and black pants. His face is bare without white paint. Viktoria looks out her front window and sees him. She throws on a black raincoat over her white dress and runs out to him in the rain. She reaches Alurich and he stops playing his musical piece. They shout in excitement so they can hear each other over the lightning and thunder echoing in the background.

VIKTORIA

What are you doing? It's pouring out here

ALURICH

Because I felt like it, I like the rain. I like to stand outside in the rain. What do you think about it?

VIKTORIA

I think you're insane. What about you're piano? It's ruined

ALURICH

I have insurance. Do you know what today is?

VIKTORIA

What? No!

ALURICH

It's the twelfth

VIKTORIA

I thought it was the thirteenth

ALURICH

No, today is the twelfth...finally

VIKTORIA
(Laughing)
Ok, unique, but different, your piano is ruined,
you're soaking wet, and all for what?

ALURICH

Tell me how it feels to be alive

VIKTORIA

What!?

ALURICH

I need to know how it feels to be alive. Tell me
how the living feel

VIKTORIA

It feels great to be alive!

ALURICH

Yes, that is right, we are the living, and it is a
great day to be alive

Alurich and Viktoria look into each other's eyes while embraced
on the rich green lawn and smile in the pouring rain. They stand
together as one, each wearing black and white, proving that love can
still exist despite their horrid worlds.

FADE TO BLACK.

Alurich Korall and Freya live as one entity. They are a married couple that has been taken hostage by the Black Coats, a top secret organization ordered to execute the citizens of their own land along with prisoners of war. The wistfully battered captives aren't given any sympathy from their treacherous commandant Colonel Hugo Snyder. Life soon turns eventful for all, as paths intertwine in a series of mishaps, murder, and mutiny. Years go by, and Alurich is drawn into an infatuation with a young beauty, Viktoria Von Buren, whose mystery haunts him. Ironically, the only steady link to their relationship is her son, Kerry, whose telepathy holds a key insight to the troubled past.

The Waking Hour is a suspense drama of biting intellect that tackles psychological principles and philosophical values. The underlying premise identifies the absurdity and danger of negative reinforcement used as a means of social propaganda. Eventually the effects take their permanent toll of cruelty towards casualty. Though extreme, universal harmony and the unity between complimentary opposites are met through symbolism of the ancient Tao. The result is a work of extraordinary and complex illustration into humanity that marks the arrival of a major new talent.

Chad Bailey is a 29 year old free-lance screenwriter. He earned a degree in film from Everest University. His hobbies include living life off the grid. He is currently writing his second screenplay.